Stories by Contemporary Writers from Shanghai

Aroma's Little Garden

This book is edited and designed by the Editorial Committee of *Cultural China* series

Text by Qin Wenjun
Translation by Tony Blishen
Cover Image by Quanjing
Interior Design by Xue Wenqing
Cover Design by Wang Wei

Copy Editor: Diane Davies
Editor: Cao Yue
Editorial Director: Zhang Yicong

Senior Consultants: Sun Yong, Wu Ying, Yang Xinci
Managing Director and Publisher: Wang Youbu

ISBN: 978-1-60220-257-3

Address any comments about *Aroma's Little Garden* to:

Better Link Press
99 Park Ave
New York, NY 10016
USA

or

Shanghai Press and Publishing Development Company, Ltd.
F 7 Donghu Road, Shanghai, China (200031)
Email: comments_betterlinkpress@hotmail.com

Printed in China by Shenzhen Donnelley Printing Co., Ltd.
1   3   5   7   9   10   8   6   4   2

Aroma's Little Garden

By Qin Wenjun
Translated by Tony Blishen

Better Link Press

Foreword

This collection of books for English readers consists of short stories and novellas published by writers based in Shanghai. Apart from a few who are immigrants to Shanghai, most of them were born in the city, from the latter part of the 1940s to the 1980s. Some of them had their works published in the late 1970s and the early 1980s; some gained recognition only in the 21st century. The older among them were the focus of the "To the Mountains and Villages" campaign in their youth, and as a result, lived and worked in the villages. The difficult paths of their lives had given them unique experiences and perspectives prior to their eventual return to Shanghai. They took up creative writing for different reasons but all share a creative urge and a love for writing. By profession, some of them are college professors, some literary editors, some directors of literary institutions, some freelance writers and some professional writers. From the individual styles of the authors and the art of their writings, readers can easily detect traces of the authors' own experiences in life, their interests, as well as their aesthetic values. Most of the works in this collection are still written in the realistic style that represents, in a painstakingly fashioned fictional world, the changes of the times in urban and rural life. Having grown up in a more open era, the younger writers have been spared the hardships experienced by their predecessors, and therefore seek greater freedom in their writing. Whatever category of writers they belong to, all of them have gained their rightful places in Chinese literary circles over the last forty years. Shanghai writers tend to favor urban narratives more than other genres of writing. Most of the works in this collection can be characterized as urban literature with Shanghai characteristics, but there are also exceptions.

Called the "Paris of the East," Shanghai was already an international metropolis in the 1920s and 30s. Being the center of China's economy, culture and literature at the time, it housed a majority of writers of importance in the history of modern Chinese literature. The list includes Lu Xun, Guo Moruo, Mao Dun and Ba Jin, who had all written and published prolifically in Shanghai. Now, with Shanghai re-emerging as a globalized metropolis, the Shanghai writers who have appeared on the literary scene in the last forty years all face new challenges and literary quests of the times. I am confident that some of the older writers will produce new masterpieces. As for the fledging new generation of writers, we naturally expect them to go far in their long writing careers ahead of them. In due course, we will also introduce those writers who did not make it into this collection.

Wang Jiren
Series Editor

Contents

Aroma Is Not Stupid

A Different Kind of Evening

Summer, the season that Aroma loved, had begun. Wild lilies opened in splendor, rushes grew in clumps, there were roses and much else and the summer scent of flowers grew richer.

As the sky cleared after the evening rain, Aroma rushed into the garden in a pretty skirt. Skirts were so good. If you stepped in a puddle there were no trouser legs to get wet.

She sucked at a sour plum iced lollipop that Auntie Mai, her nurse, had bought her. Her tongue was like a block of ice and the wind blew gently on her legs. She saw a cloud of dragonflies, perhaps their wings were damp from the rain and they flew more slowly. Aroma liked the dragonflies, she waved her lollipop in the air and said, "Miss Dragonfly, please have an iced lolly."

Aroma still wanted to see how it was that dragonflies could fly. It must be wonderful to have wings. But the dragonflies were shy and like small aeroplanes flew higher and further away. However, a fly came by. Aroma did not like dirty flies and put the lollipop in her mouth but the greedy fly licked at her pretty finger.

In a while, Aroma noticed a strange looking flower in the garden. She went over to smell its scent when all of a sudden the flower sprang into life. It was actually a grasshopper, but it wasn't a green grasshopper, it was a pink one. Aroma went to ask Auntie Mai why this was so. Auntie Mai said, "Wait until you go to school, you'll find out then."

"Will I find it all out in first year primary?" asked Aroma.

Auntie Mai said, "After you've been to school you'll be properly educated like other girls. You won't be a wild child anymore."

Aroma suddenly asked, "Auntie Mai, did you do first year primary?"

Auntie Mai said, "Of course I did. We learned to write characters: large, small, many, few ... up, down, come, go."

"When you did first year primary did you learn about grasshoppers not being the same?"

"You really are a stupid child. The things that need to be learned in this world are so many they can't be counted," said Auntie Mai loftily.

"I'm not a stupid child, I can see with my own eyes," Aroma said to herself.

Aroma saw that the pink grasshopper had got into the thick shrubbery and so followed it in. She saw it pause for a long time, motionless. She also saw another, green, grasshopper jumping about in the grass as if it were practicing the high jump. Aroma felt she had found the answer and shouted, "I've found out, I've found out!"

When Auntie Mai saw Aroma emerge from the shrubbery covered in damp grass seed, her knees and elbows black with dirt and her body covered in spiders' webs, she couldn't help bursting out, "You're so unlike a proper girl. Wild, wild child!"

"I'm called Aroma, not wild child," said Aroma angrily. She considered her name the best. It was because her mother and father loved her that they had chosen such a fine name for her.

Why was it that Auntie Mai didn't understand Aroma?

"I think this grasshopper isn't the same as others," said Aroma, "pink grasshoppers definitely like flowers and green ones like grass."

"Huh," said Auntie Mai, "whatever next, stupid child, there'll be brown grasshoppers in the fields as well."

"Really? I'll go and look for brown grasshoppers, they probably like mud." Aroma made for the shrubbery as she spoke but Auntie Mai pulled her back, saying, "You're forbidden to be a wild child."

Aroma's mother heard and said, "Our Aroma isn't a wild child, it's just that she's not the same as other children."

Aroma looked up and asked, "Mum, do you still like me even though I'm not the same as other children?"

"Of course I like you," said her mother kindly, "you're very special and very lovable."

Aroma was delighted, and relieved. She thought, "Why should everything be the same? Some grasshoppers grow to the color of grass and some to the color of flowers and nobody said that they couldn't. There are some girls who like flowers and some who like grass, some girls are lovable, some clever, some pretty and some gentle, so it's all right to be different."

Before supper, Didi, Aroma's naughty younger brother, had brought back three dragonflies to keep in a jar. Aroma observed them carefully through half-closed eyes. They were not the same. One was light green and one had transparent wings, like the wind. Aroma had never seen the color of the wind but thought that it was bound to be transparent. The third dragonfly was grey with bright wings that seemed embroidered with silver. "You're not all the same but I like you. You're all lovable," she said.

Aroma brought the dragonflies in under her own mosquito net to play for a while, as if they were guests. She allowed them to fly wherever they liked within the net and told them about her father's business trip and told them too that she was shortly to become a primary schoolgirl and knew the way to school already. Flying about in the garden and playing in the water all day how could the dragonflies know about all these fresh events?

It grew dark at the approach of the real night. Aroma lifted her mosquito net and let the dragonflies go. She thought that perhaps they were tired from playing and were waiting to go home. Their moments of departure varied as well. The light green dragonfly flew off at once, it seemed impetuous by nature. Neither fast nor slow, the grey one took two leisurely circuits within the net, showing that it was in no great hurry and that it would be no bad thing to have another look round.

The remaining dragonfly with the transparent wings seemed in no way lonely and waited for a long time on the mosquito net until a breath of wind arrived that shook the net from side to side, when it took off. Obviously it had been waiting to catch the breeze.

"Goodbye dragonflies. Goodbye dragonfly playmates."

Aroma watched the three beautiful dragonflies fly, fly nonchalantly away, and knew that summer was the season that both she and they enjoyed.

That night Aroma snuggled under her mosquito net, thinking still about the three dragonflies and later falling asleep in the land of dreams. With the dragonflies as company Aroma passed a peaceful, different night and dreamed different dreams.

At Sea

Aroma's father was going on a business trip to the other side of the sea. He was going on a ship.

When Aroma's nurse, Auntie Mai, heard that her father was going across the sea on a ship she told him to be careful of seasickness. She said that on a boat, even if there were no big waves, there would be small ones and the boat would rock. That was because the sea was rough and rose and fell. It was unpredictable as well.

Aroma had never seen the sea and asked, "Dad, is there the smell of fish in the sea?"

"There is, definitely," said Dad.

Aroma said, "Dad, the sea smells of whales and dolphins. Dad, you must take me to see more of the sea!"

"All right, I'll help you listen to the sea as well," he said.

The day Dad left Mum gave him some Tiger Balm ointment and Auntie Mai gave him some dried radishes. Dad was delighted. He liked the family to be concerned for him and to be sensitive on this point.

After he left, Aroma often took her younger brother to the mouth of the alley to wait for their father to come home. She thought that her father's ship would come steaming in at once and that it was very, very close. But Auntie Mai said that Aroma was a stupid child because Dad had telephoned and said that he was still on the other side of the sea.

Aroma missed her father and so turned the house into the ocean and made his large bed into a ship. In this way she and her brother could "swim" like fish in the "sea" and they could get on board "Dad's boat" any time they liked.

Auntie Mai accompanied them while they played. She told Aroma that Dad liked children a lot and it just so happened that Mum liked children as well, and so they had Aroma and her younger brother. This had been arranged by the previous generation.

"Why did the previous generation make this arrangement and not some other arrangement?" asked Aroma.

Auntie Mai said, "Don't ask. Nobody can explain it properly. When I think of it, my heart is so empty I feel like crying."

Aroma didn't understand what Auntie Mai was saying but dared not ask, afraid that she would call her "stupid child" again. In her mind, Aroma mulled over what Auntie Mai had said and suddenly though that if Dad and Mum had never met, Dad would have been somebody else's father. Like Auntie Mai, Aroma's heart was so empty she felt like crying. But after a while she forgot these painful ideas because Dad really was her own dad and that was really good.

Every day Aroma waited for her father to come home but when he eventually did Aroma wasn't there. She was in the garden looking at a sunflower. Dad strode in and was discovered first by the child who lived at the mouth of the alley who shouted, "A good dad's back."

Then all the children at the mouth of the alley took up the cry, "Someone's good dad is back."

When Aroma and Didi heard, they rushed up and hugged

their father tightly. Close against her father, Aroma noticed a salty tang to his shirt and said to her brother, "Dad's brought back the smell of the sea as well."

"There's the sea breeze too, hidden in my pocket," said Dad, "put your hand in and feel it."

Dad had brought back half a jar of white sand from the other side of the sea and he taught Aroma and the others the calls of seabirds and the sound of the wind at sea. In the photographs he had taken there were the houses on the other side of the sea and trees and people and the life over there.

Afterwards Dad said boastfully to Mum, "Such prestige! Bathed in the reflected glory of my daughter and son the progress of my return was widely reported. They said, 'A good dad has returned in glory.'"

"That's enough. It's not as if you're the emperor," said Mum laughing.

Dad was the best dad of all. He had brought back lovely presents from the other side of the sea: a big bag of sweets shaped like cowrie shells for Aroma to share with her younger brother. He had also bought the specialty of the area: a pair of vases with sunflowers on them, the flower that Aroma liked most of all, inlaid on a deep blue ground. Glass was the local product but Dad had specially chosen the sunflower. Aroma was the treasure of Dad's heart and that was where he also kept the flower she loved.

Dad had also brought back animal toys made of very transparent glass for Aroma and her brother. He had bought Mum a cloisonné bracelet and for Auntie Mai there was a box of northern fried dough twists.

He proudly said that the boat had encountered a force seven gale and some passengers had been seasick, staggering all over the place. He had used the Tiger Balm ointment and radishes to help the seasick passengers but he himself had been completely unaffected. Excellent, excellent.

Dad also brought back with him the joy of a family reunited

after separation, a scene that, for Aroma, became a memory of happiness.

A Concert of Raindrops

One day, Mr. Wood, their neighbor, invited all the children including Aroma to his house.

Mr. Wood's name was not actually Wood but "wood" formed part of the character for his name. When neighbors called him Mr. Wood they were also teasing him a little because he was slow, but he was a good man and happy too. He loved birds and had five that he could not bear to keep in a cage but raised inside the house. There were bats in the rafters as well, rather as if the birds and the bats were friends with each other.

When Aroma and the others came through the door they saw five large food dishes on the table. The birds ate at the table as if they were Mr. Wood's children. They pecked away happily but unlike children they stood in the dish to eat using their claws as chopsticks, flicking things aside and sometimes sending the food flying.

"After you've eaten your fill, go and take a rest in your iron bedroom," said Mr. Wood to the little birds, speaking to them as if they were part of his own family and going on to say, "why kill time stuck in the dining room?"

The five birds truly understood what he was saying, spread their wings, circled above Aroma and the other children's heads a couple of times and then flew off to their little iron coop.

Mr. Wood lived on the ground floor with a small yard outside where there was a small, very low, iron-framed coop with glass sides which made it bright inside. The most interesting thing about the iron coop was that there was a little well in it. Next to the little well was a bonsai pot with a tree in it with forked branches that extended into the iron coop and on which the birds had made their nests. The crown of the tree poked through the roof of the iron coop like a protective umbrella. The floor of the coop was covered in a cushion of dried reeds and petals.

"Shall we sit on the cushion? That way we can get a scent of the outdoors," said Mr. Wood.

"Does the iron coop have a name?" asked Aroma.

Mr. Wood said, "Yes, it does. A new one every day. When the sun is out, it's called Warmth, when the wind blows it's called Unquiet. What's it called now? It's called Welcome Fairy Guests."

"It's great fun here," said Aroma. "Mr. Wood, are you happy every day?"

Mr. Wood said, "I'm learning from the birds. They are small and weak but they're still happy in the face of storm and snow. How beautiful they look when they fly."

"It's raining," shouted somebody outside, accompanied by the sound of hurried footsteps. People were rushing to find shelter to avoid the falling rain.

Mr. Wood said, "Excellent, we'll have an opportunity to enjoy a concert of raindrops."

"Raindrop music?" everybody asked in astonishment.

Ping ping pong pong the raindrops fell, sounding a monotonous *ting ting tong tong* on the roof of the iron coop. Aroma's brother asked, "How come it sounds like a leaking tap?"

Mr. Wood said, "Hold your breath, prick up your ears and listen quietly to the music."

Aroma listened to the sound of the rain on the little coop, there was something brittle about it, but she heard all sorts of sounds every day. Could they be called music?

"Quiet, breath in deeply, listen to the rhythm of that lovely tinkling tune: *di da da di di di da*, the rain fairy is coming to the mountains ... *di da da di di di da*," Mr. Wood beat out the rhythm of the raindrops.

Aroma kept quiet and inwardly beat out the rhythm. Of course, the sound of the raindrops on the roof of the iron coop was beautiful, one moment it was a crisp *ding ding dong dong*, the next it seemed like the music of a zither plucking at the heartstrings.

"Listen, this time it's a kind of stop and start string and flute sound as if the rain's thinking of something sad and is crying," Mr. Wood sighed. "It's beautiful, really beautiful."

Truly, Aroma was enchanted. An indistinct joy flecked with sadness had entered her, as if a bird with beating wings had sown the seed from its beak into the fields of her tiny heart.

Mr. Wood said, "Look, the birds are drunk with the sound of it. They are so happy, it's the sound of beautiful music in their hearts."

That afternoon was unforgettable. Together, Mr. Wood and Aroma and the other children had listened carefully to the fleeting beauty that had arrived with the rain. Beating time to the raindrops the children had eaten the egg rolls that Mr. Wood had cooked. Sometimes they sang, sometimes they were happy, sometimes they were thoughtful and sometimes they did nothing at all and sat quietly with the five little birds listening to the raindrops falling on the roof of the iron coop: music that was beyond the power of speech to describe.

The five little birds were happy. Did they too think that the beauty of the sound of raindrops falling to earth was something that could be deeply felt? The birds also seemed to experience the peace and magnificence of the world, even in the narrow confines of their iron coop.

The rain stopped suddenly. How Aroma hoped that these moments of beauty would last and last. As the children said goodbye to Mr. Wood the music in Aroma's heart continued to play and for a long time Aroma was able to make out the tune in the rain. Sometimes, when Aroma woke up in the early morning dew, she discovered the rhythm of rain beating in her heart. Sometimes, when she walked in the dew in the garden and heard the birds singing she felt that she existed in a golden world of music.

Aroma always hoped that Mr. Wood would invite the children again. One day, Auntie Mai told her that Mr. Wood had been unlucky in life. This made Aroma respect Mr. Wood, living with his five birds, even more. He bore the burdens of a troubled mind but still had the ability to spread happiness and to find the beauty and joy of life.

Princess Books

Aroma joined first year primary. It was the literature and language lessons that she liked most because the teacher often read them stories. Aroma liked the stories about princesses even though a princess wasn't as pretty or powerful as the empress who was a married grown-up without any mysterious glory. The princess was like a mysterious star, a scented lily. Moreover, one day a handsome prince would come to seek her hand and she would wear a beautiful wedding dress. What fun that would be.

Aroma made her father buy her books about princesses. Her father was delighted and bought her a whole pile of them. Aroma read the books and was enchanted. One day she suddenly thought that she would build a palace and live in it like a princess.

The palace wasn't built at home because her little brother would smash it up. He wasn't interested in stories about princesses and liked to play battle and pirate games.

Aroma found a playmate in Duidui, a pretty little girl who also wanted to play at being a princess.

"There can be two princesses in a palace," said Aroma. "Let's build a palace at your home."

"Good, good," said Duidui, "all the grown-ups are out."

Duidui's family lived on the floor above Aroma. Aroma marked out an area on the floor of the big room as the site of the palace and then brought in the flowers from the balcony, flowerpot by flowerpot, because princesses should always have flowers to enjoy. Then she arranged the high-backed chairs in two rows to act as the princesses' ladies in waiting and erected a pavilion on the bed. Then, thinking the bed too high to climb up and down from, she arranged the quilt on the floor as a staircase.

This staircase was soft but better than no staircase at all, and in any case no palace could be without a staircase.

The palace was already beginning to look quite something and Aroma called Duidui to join her in being a princess but Duidui refused. She wanted to build a palace to her own design. After all, she was a princess too. She said, "The palace I want isn't like this. I would like a lotus pool. If there's a lotus pool in the palace I can stand facing the lotus flowers and comb my hair."

Who was to say "no"? Aroma said, "All right, I want to dance in the lotus pool."

Duidui brought in a wooden pail, put in some plastic flowers, added two buckets of water and in the twinkling of an eye, there was a lotus pool. "The lotus pool's really beautiful," she shouted happily. "This is where the princess combs her hair as she's looking at the lotus flowers. I want to make another big pool that both princesses can dance in, all right?"

Aroma thought that another lotus pool would be fine. The princess could comb her hair facing the lotus flowers and could also dance with them. The two girls, puffing *heyho heyho*, dragged in a large wooden tub and, like Hercules, carried in several pails of water and poured them into the tub. But the tub leaked and in an instant it overflowed and there was water everywhere, splashing wherever you walked.

"What are we going to do?" Duidui asked anxiously. "Our palaces look like the sea."

"What fun," Aroma had a sudden idea and said, "we simply add more water and we can be princesses in the Dragon Palace. How about that?"

"I'll do what you say," said Duidui, "but it'll need more water before it looks as if the Dragon King lives there."

So as to be princesses in the Dragon Palace as soon as they could, Aroma and Duidui poured bucket after bucket of water into the room, but the water level didn't rise. It was very odd, as if there was a monster swallowing it all. Aroma was not to be defeated and continued to pour water on to the floor. At that very moment she heard her brother shouting, "Help! There's a flood coming in!" The water in Duidui's home had seeped through to the room below and caused catastrophic flooding in Aroma's home.

Aroma felt that she had missed out. She hadn't been able to be a princess and had just been carrying and pouring water. Her clothes were wet through and her hair was a mess. Worst of all, Auntie Mai had called her "Stupid child" again.

When her father came home in the evening and saw that the family's quilts and all the clothes in the wardrobe were wet, he sat there in a mood and said that Aroma was the "princess of trouble."

Aroma was upset and afraid that her father wouldn't buy her any more books about princesses. But that was not what Dad did. Instead he said, "In future don't be a princess of trouble."

Her father still bought books about princesses for Aroma and her interest grew and grew and she began to want to read other books. Later on she still caused trouble but less and less because princesses had to be elegant and dignified.

Gobstoppers

Spring had arrived and the grass was especially green, like the strokes of a character written by Aroma with a green brush. Aroma rushed into the garden to recite her lessons as soon as it was light, sniffing the scent of the grass as she did so. Mum said that Aroma's name really meant the aroma of mint.

Aroma breathed in the spring air deeply and her whole body lightened as if it would soon float away. Her tiny head was in a daze and she felt like somebody else, like the princess of the garden. When Dad came looking for her he found her sound asleep in the shrubbery like a kitten.

Dad said, "Only small animals sleep as soundly as you do."

"Why?"

"Because they have no troubles."

Aroma said, "I've seen a pink grasshopper. It was beautiful, perhaps it had no troubles either?"

Dad said, "I've never seen a pink grasshopper but I know from books that poisonous grasshoppers are brightly colored as a warning to people to keep away from them. Nature is wonderful. It changes all the time but it has its own rules doesn't it?"

Aroma asked, "Dad, why do people have troubles?"

"Time to go, we shall be late. You have to go to school."

"Are children who fall asleep reciting lessons stupid children?" Aroma asked anxiously.

"They are, they are," said Auntie Mai from the side.

Dad said, "You have to remember that children get cleverer by going to school ..."

Aroma was hurt and felt that nobody loved her. After walking on for a long while she again asked, "Why do you get clever by going to school?"

"You learn the ability to do things."

"If a child was in a different place would it learn different things?"

Dad didn't have a chance to answer. They had arrived at the school. He saw Aroma to the entrance and watched her go in through the door.

Aroma entered the classroom rather in the manner of a balloon. Little Ox, who shared a desk with her, asked, "Why are you so pleased with yourself?"

Little Ox was fed up with Aroma because Duidui had said that Aroma was braver than he was. He couldn't stand this and was unwilling to give in to Aroma on this point. At that moment, a large spider came hanging down from the ceiling. Little Ox grabbed it and thrust it under Aroma's nose, saying, "Scare yourself to death!"

Aroma took the spider in her hand and said to it, "Little thing, you aren't frightening at all, you're lovable. You know the spiders in the garden. I've planted a sunflower there. Go and call on them. The spiders there are the best sort, the thread they spin is strong and sticks to the insects' feet, and the mosquitoes get all tied up. There's a spider king there who can eat twenty mosquitoes in a day."

"Aroma, you're amazing!" interjected Duidui in surprised awe. Duidui had dark brown eyes, a mouth like a cherry and normally liked to wear a red hat. She had great respect for Aroma's courage and even in her dreams tried to be as brave as Aroma but had not yet learned how because every time she thought of something sad she would immediately burst into tears. The music teacher said that she would be best as an actress.

After school Aroma took the spider home to the garden. The windows of her home overlooked the little garden and looked nearly due west where there was a beautiful large magnolia tree whose thick green foliage gave shade from the direct rays of the sun so that the soil beneath the windows was quite moist and sprouted all kinds of wild grasses and plants whose names she did not know, like the scallion that grew up so straight. Amongst them was a beautiful, graceful sunflower which she had planted the previous year.

Aroma saw that her sunflower was dancing, delicately waving in the direction of the sun. Next day, Aroma told Little Ox of her discovery. Little Ox not only refused to believe her but told others that she was the queen of boasters.

Her classmates also said that they had never seen a dancing sunflower. Unable to find approval or recognition Aroma was reluctant to go to school. Having not gone for a day and then another, on the third day she simply dare not go at all for fear that the teacher would not accept her. She thought sadly to herself, "I can only be a stupid truant child" and burst into broken-hearted tears.

Aroma's father discovered this and wanted to send her to school saying that the teacher had already forgiven her. But Aroma particularly did not want to lose face and was frightened that if she did go to school Little Ox and the others would mock her. Her father was determined that Aroma should not be cowardly and should face up to the challenge.

Dad thought of a way to deal with this and prepared two kinds of sweet for her: one soft, the other big and hard. Dad whispered a few words in Aroma's ear.

Aroma went to school in a panic. Duidui asked her, "Why haven't you been to school, huh?"

Saying "Have a sweet," Aroma quickly stuffed a soft sweet into Duidui's mouth.

Little Ox was really unfriendly. He looked at Aroma and said, "Here comes the queen of boasters!"

Aroma didn't argue with him and said, "Here, have a sweet," and stuffed a hard sweet into his mouth. Little Ox sucked on the sweet and carried on asking, "Did you dare not come to school?"

"Have another sweet," said Aroma, stuffing yet another sweet into his mouth.

Aroma recalled that Dad had said that these sweets were called "gobstoppers." They were very effective and after a few questions Little Ox gave up and later even forgot Aroma's "criminal record." Using Dad's method Aroma regained her dignity and went back to school where she sat in the classroom, filled with love of her class.

Some weeks later a hospital colleague of Duidui's mother, a doctor called Little Dumpling, came to visit the family. He heard Duidui describe how Auntie Mai had scolded Aroma as a stupid child and also how every day Aroma hoped that the sunflower would dance. Dr. Little Dumpling made a point of telling Aroma's family that there really were plants that could dance. It was the effect of photosynthesis.

Aroma was delighted and breathed a sigh of relief, thinking in her little head, "Perhaps my sunflower is tired, the same as people are." Sunflowers couldn't dance all the time. Not every plant could dance. There were some that couldn't and some that weren't brave enough. But the world would be even more beautiful if there were more that could.

Later everybody realized that sunflowers could "dance" now and then. Little Ox discovered that he had been mistaken and copied Aroma's method and bought some sweets thinking to use them as "gobstoppers." But Aroma uttered not a word of criticism of Little Ox. She realized that both boys and girls needed face.

Consequently, Little Ox had no use for the gobstoppers and ate the whole bag himself. However, from then on the tone of his arguments with Aroma was not as nasty as before.

Sweetheart the Kitten

One Sunday afternoon, just as Aroma's family were having tea, an uninvited guest rushed in: a very dirty little kitten with bedraggled fur which, nevertheless, at once made itself at home. Aroma fed it some tidbits and it rubbed itself against her legs in a gesture of greedy friendship.

Dad looked at the kitten and said, "It's got a collar, it belongs to some other family and has got lost."

He opened the door and ushered the kitten out. After all, who was to object? It ought to return to its own home. The kitten marched down the steps outside the door and, as it crossed the courtyard, arched its back and took an interested turn over the plank bridge across the lotus pond and back, and then turned and rushed out of the entrance. Not far off it met a workman calling, "Mend any old beds!"

The workman's voice was loud and filled the narrow alleyway. The kitten changed its mind, turned and charged back into Aroma's home. Dad still wanted to take it to find its own home but it stuck to the ground like a leech and only after Dad had left did it stretch out a paw and pull at Aroma's slippers that were embroidered with a row of handsome fish.

Everybody could see that the kitten wanted very much to be Aroma's family cat.

Mum took off the kitten's collar and gave it a bubble bath

with as much care as washing wool. The kitten stretched its paws and waved and in a while a handsome cat emerged from the dirty black soap bubbles. It was just like a toy cat with thick fur and a short tail with a dash of yellow at the end.

Aroma picked up the kitten and held it against her, its body was soft and warm. It enjoyed Aroma's embrace and its paws rested gently on her shoulders. Later her brother and her mother came and held it. Aroma called it Sweetheart.

Sweetheart became the baby of the family. Its miaow was soft and sweet and it was both small and lovable. Like a princess, the luxury-loving Sweetheart relished a life lived in the dry sweet smelling warmth of a den of quilts. It liked to eat rice in fish soup in small mouthfuls and sometimes sat sadly staring into the mirror. It particularly liked to keep its nose clean, wiping its face time and again as if it was aware that its face was handsome and should be kept clean for the sake of dignity and respect.

Sweetheart was also a lazy rascal and when Mum and Aroma went to the market and wanted to take it along, it played up and climbed into the vegetable basket that Mum was carrying and went to sleep. It also liked to jump into Aroma's lap when she was reading and lie across the book, looking slyly at the illustrations. It liked Aroma's brother to whirl round and round while holding it tightly. It liked a lot of guests to visit and distinguished company and going for a walk in the garden with Dad to look at the moon.

All the family loved Sweetheart because Dad said that if anybody in the family kicked it, and others saw it, they would come and kick it too. It was the same for the family cat as it was for the family itself: only the total love of the family would make other people more than careful.

Sweetheart was grateful for benefits received and regarded itself as a member of the family. It would dance every evening for them. Its favorite dance was to whirl round and chase that little bit of yellow on the tip of its tail.

How round was the moon on the evening of the Mid-autumn Festival? Aroma tied a handkerchief into the shape of a mouse and gave it to Sweetheart who was beyond delight and danced curled like a ball of wool. Sweetheart's joy lighted Aroma's heart like a lamp.

Just then an unfamiliar voice outside the window said, "Anybody at home? I've come looking for a lost kitten."

It was a stranger with a long nose and a bald head who said that his family kitten had been lost for a while. He had heard that it had landed up here.

Dad invited the man in to look at the cat but Sweetheart was not to be found anywhere.

That night, when Aroma went to fetch her pyjamas she heard a sort of snoring sound. Sweetheart was asleep hidden in the wardrobe. As Aroma watched, Sweetheart opened her mouth in satisfaction and emitted a great yawn.

The man came again the following day and after looking carefully shook his head and said that it wasn't his family's kitten.

Aroma wept tears of joy and her brother cried too, so much that the veins on the side of his head bulged like earthworms, but Sweetheart was calmer than all of them and quickly learned how to carry slippers in her mouth for the family.

Several months later, at the end of the year, a car suddenly pulled up outside Aroma's home and a very good-looking lady descended from it.

It was no joke this time. The lady had brought the cat mother. The cat mother was called Mary, a very superior looking animal with whiter fur, thicker and finer, like a cat in an expensive fur coat.

Mary took not a bit of notice of Aroma and was very stuck up. But the cat mother and Sweetheart were as alike as two peas in a pod and had the same patch of yellow at the tips of their tails.

"My little Mary. I've been looking for you every day," said the good-looking lady.

"No way, Sweetheart likes it here," snarled Aroma's brother.

Aroma clung to Sweetheart in floods of tears and would not

let go however much she was urged.

At this moment the good-looking lady's daughter arrived. She was very small and walked as if she were dragged by something. She thrust between people's legs to embrace Aroma's knees and said, coaxingly, "Elder sister, I want my cat. Please let me have her back."

The little girl looked pure and angelic. Her name was Jenni.

Aroma obediently gave the cat to Jenni and her brother agreed. He was a very different boy with all the pride of a male.

The good-looking lady put a new collar on Sweetheart, who squeaked unwillingly, and Aroma quickly gave her the mouse she had made out of a handkerchief, which Sweetheart then held in her mouth.

The car started and Sweetheart, with her paws against the rear window, gazed dumbly at Aroma, Dad, Mum and little brother as if trying to fix them in her memory.

It was only when the car had started that Aroma discovered the handkerchief mouse lying on the ground. That night Aroma wouldn't let the door be closed and waited for Sweetheart to come searching for the handkerchief mouse. Dad let her have her way and this time Auntie Mai didn't say that Aroma was a stupid girl.

Sweetheart was just a little cat in Aroma's life but Dad later said that Aroma had grown up and now understood the price of love.

The Garden Princess

The Garden Princess

At the beginning of spring the sound of thunder awakened the plants and the grass and they emerged on tiptoe. Once they had become lush and green the whole earth changed and became baking hot. Summer had arrived. The wild lilies opened in beauty, there were clumps of rushes and roses too, and the summer scent of flowers was relaxing and deeply fragrant.

Sometimes Aroma woke very early, just as it was getting light and rushed out to the little garden that she had made, and while she recited her lessons by heart she counted the flowers to see if any more had opened. As she recited, she smelt wave upon wave of the sweet scent of flowers and quickly became light-headed, with a wonderful feeling of floating like a balloon.

Beyond the windows of Aroma's home there was a garden that was used by several neighboring families and beneath the window of her own home she had surrounded a small patch of ground with a ring of smooth pebbles. This was her own little garden.

The lesson text was called "A Bunch of Flowers" but however she recited it she felt it hard to say. Then she had a sudden idea and sang the lesson to a tune of her own that she liked:

"Little flower, little flower

How beautiful your scented petals are ..."

Aroma's mood improved as she sang.

Sung with such heartfelt sincerity the elegant words were unforgettable.

At that moment she saw an extraordinary sight. She had planted several sunflowers in her little garden. One of them had grown particularly tall, in a flowerpot, with pairs of leaves and stems and a fine main stalk, and as Aroma sang her song the sunflower began to sway gently from the waist in time with her singing.

Aroma leant forward and gently tugged a leaf, saying, "Little flower, little flower take my hand and sing."

And so the sunflower gently danced its willowy dance.

"Little flower, little flower, what joy to dance together ..."

Aroma sang the song a number of times and danced with the sunflower then. She felt that she had become the "princess of the country of the little garden."

The "princess of the country of the little garden" ought by right to live on a tree leaf and if she wants to swim she should find a drop of pure dew.

Dad came out and seeing Aroma fast asleep, whispered tenderly, "It must be a little dog, or perhaps a kitten, only a little animal could sleep so soundly."

In a while, the call of a bird woke Aroma with a start.

Dad said, "Aroma, time for school, it's where all children have to go."

"Why? We aren't all the same, let the ones that want to go."

"Can't be done," said Dad.

Aroma didn't want to go to school because she didn't like reciting by heart, didn't like it being the same every day, didn't like being worried and didn't like having to go to school when she had thoughts she didn't like on her mind.

However, when she actually got to school and saw the familiar buildings and playground and the trees and grass her dislike flew away, her footsteps quickened and she imagined that she was a butterfly flying into the classroom from on high, and that everybody, including Little Ox who she shared a desk with, was down below and had to look up in order to see her.

Little Ox snorted when he saw her. He rather despised girls and often liked to frighten Aroma. This time, he grabbed a big spider, put it on Aroma's desk saying, "Here's a present for you!"

Aroma was not to be frightened. She bent down to look, the

tip of her nose almost touching the spider, calling it "little thing" and feeling that this present wasn't in the least scary. In fact, it was rather sweet and so she said, "Little spider, come on to my hand and I will take you to a really high tree."

Duidui saw and thought Aroma was terrific. Duidui was very pretty, like a snow white princess. But strangely, sometimes she was timid and at other times bold. Sometimes she was happy and at other times miserable. The moment she thought of something sad she would burst into tears. Perhaps it would be best if she became an actress when she grew up.

Duidui and Aroma were neighbors and got on all right. Duidui had great respect for Aroma's courage and said that she was a tomboy.

Little Ox said, "But she tells fibs. She said that she had planted a sunflower that could dance."

"But it does dance."

"Make it dance so that I can see. Huh, tigress, you don't need any practice in fibbing."

"Say that again."

"I don't want to," said Little Ox who did not like to lose face. He was a little frightened to see Aroma glaring fiercely at him and dared not provoke her. However, he didn't want to admit that it was unwise to provoke Aroma and said that he was not going to take orders from her because she was a nasty little girl. Girls who were rather nasty were tigresses. It was only girls who were not nasty who were little lambs.

"You're a paper tiger," said Aroma.

Little Ox was furious. He did not give in, how could a boy be beaten by a girl? And he burst out again. A little later Teacher Chen came into the classroom and heard Little Ox and Aroma rowing interminably, neither giving in to the other.

"False accusation!"

"Queen Liar!"

"False accusation!"

Teacher Chen heard them and said, "What's this? Stop it, both of you!"

Little Ox said, "She says she has a sunflower that can dance."

Aroma explained, "Teacher Chen, my sunflower really can dance, I've seen it. To prove it, come home with me after school and see."

"All right, let Duidui go with you after school and she can tell everybody what she has seen."

Later Teacher Chen made Aroma recite "A Bunch of Flowers" and Aroma asked, "Can I sing it?"

"This isn't a music lesson, you know," interrupted Little Ox.

Aroma could sing the words, but if she had to recite it, phrase by phrase, she stammered between one phrase and the next because she needed to sing it in her head first.

"Every little flower
Comes from somewhere
Little flower, little flower
How beautiful your scented petals are
Little flower, little flower
What joy to dance together ..."

Teacher Chen shook her head vigorously saying, "What 'what joy to dance together'? It's all over the place. That line's not in the book."

"Little flower, little flower
Take my hand and sing ..."

"Right, you have to learn this properly," said Teacher Chen.

Aroma was upset, but she still dreamed that if only Teacher Chen knew that she had planted a sunflower that could dance she would definitely get a smile from her tomorrow.

Things Do Not Go According to Plan

After school Aroma trotted back to her little garden where there was a very special sunflower that could actually dance.

Singing loudly Aroma danced to the sunflower.

She tried countless times and as long as she sang to it loudly and from the heart, whether or not it was the reciting song she had made up or songs from the radio, it listened intently.

Then, swaying from its narrow waist, it coolly turned its round, round flowered disc in time to the music. There were times when the music stopped and, as if it had a song in its heart, it humbly danced a revolving dance as it faced the sun.

Aroma looked everywhere but alas, Duidui was not around. Duidui performed dance steps as she walked and, unlike Aroma, never walked as fast as the wind itself. At that moment Aroma saw a very tall man walk into Springwater Lane, as if he were a stranger crossing the road. He stood, looking to left and right, and at once she waved to him, "Uncle."

She told this unknown uncle her good news. He looked at her and replied, "Yes, I saw."

"Perhaps a lot of plants like dancing but haven't learnt how to," Aroma continued conversationally.

"Uh," replied the uncle.

"When this sunflower has seeds I can plant them everywhere. It will be really good for the world to have dancing flowers and maybe every child can have one," said Aroma.

However, the uncle had taken a turn round Springwater Lane and then left. He was now out of sight.

At this point, Aroma's younger brother rushed up, seized the radio and turned the knob to tune it to the Chinese opera program which was just broadcasting a local Shanghai comic opera duologue. Some comedian or other was repeating the Suzhou dialect phrase *miaogen duye*, which means "Miaogen's dad," from a traditional song with exaggerated tones as a sort of catchphrase. This duologue was different to the Northern kind where one character played both parts. *Miaogen duye* was a kind of lament.

The radio repeated *miaogen duye* again and Didi chuckled and savored the phrase on his tongue: "*Miaogen duye.*"

"Horrible, really horrible," said Aroma.

"It's good, it is really," said Didi defensively with his two little hands on the top of his head in a funny imitation of some strange animal as he mouthed *miaogen duye* ...

Aroma was fed up but there was nothing that she could do because Didi thought that this was the way to make her like him.

In a while Duidui drifted into sight. The moment she arrived Didi pulled in his horns. This young man liked to appear sophisticated in front of pretty girls and did not want to be found lacking in manners.

Duidui was a little uncertain as she arrived at the little garden, and looked up at the verandah of her apartment. She lived on the second floor where there were a lot of windows that faced the sun and everybody could look down into the garden. However, her grandfather had asked a workman to take out the central window and put in a little balcony. The balcony had ornamental railings and jutted out with just enough room to stand on. She loved to stand on the balcony as if she were suspended there.

The windows of the families on the first floor also looked out onto the common garden but they did not have the resources to construct such a floating balcony.

Aroma's apartment was on the ground floor. The windows faced slightly westwards where there was a beautiful, large magnolia tree with luxuriant foliage that shaded her apartment from the direct rays of the sun.

The little garden that she had built beneath the largest and most central of her apartment's windows was quite damp and had lots of attractive green plants with names that she did not know, all planted by the family. Some stood as straight as scallion and some stood delicately bowed so that Aroma didn't like to pick them. She had also planted five elegant sunflowers and the little garden looked like a small patch of open countryside.

Only the most handsome sunflower in the middle could dance. It was also the tallest.

After Duidui arrived they sang and danced together but no matter how good the song was the sunflower wouldn't dance again.

"I know how," Aroma was not in the least discouraged and

took the radio from Didi and leant on the windowsill with it. Usually, she liked to lean over the windowsill and talk to the sunflowers below. The windowsill was fine. You could stand there and look up at the sky without being dazzled.

But on this evening, although Aroma broadcast a soprano singing as well as dance music, the sunflower didn't dance.

"Aiya, aiya," said Duidui, "that's odd, really odd."

Records of Absence

Next day, as usual, Dad took Aroma to school from Springwater Lane and then went off to work. The moment Dad had gone Aroma left too and returned to the little garden country.

Auntie Mai realized that Aroma was playing truant but still looked on her kindly. She made her two seafood omelets from shrimps, eggs and flour as well as meatball and radish soup, a really delicious meal. Auntie Mai was there every day. She wasn't a member of Aroma's family and other people said that she was a "servant" but whatever the case, in all matters of household and housekeeping it was she to whom everybody turned. "Aroma," she said, "children like fun. By all means play for a day but you must have a change of heart tomorrow and go to school."

Aroma spent the day at home like a cat and in a while visited her sunflowers in the little garden country. Remembering that it was still spring, she soaked seeds in water, drilled several small holes and planted the seeds in them. Some sunflowers sprouted in three days but one took a week, as if it were over-sleeping.

Later they all grew together with leaves in pairs. Aroma weeded them, got rid of the insects, sang to them and watered them. Dad helped by putting on manure. Aroma couldn't remember from which day it was but the sunflower that could dance grew furiously, spiraling up higher and higher, incomparably beautiful, like the handsome elder sister of the other sunflowers.

"Little flower, little flower

How beautiful your scented petals are
Little flower, little flower
Take my hand and sing
Little flower, little flower
What joy to dance together."

But the loudly singing Aroma had not noticed something strange: the sunflower would not do its revolving dance at all.

"Little flower, little flower why are you unhappy? Does your back ache?"

Aroma found a little bamboo stick as a support, saying, "Never mind, lean on this."

In fact, Aroma was worried. Unless the sunflower danced once more, there was no way she could go back to school because she couldn't prove to everybody that she hadn't told a lie.

Little Ox would make fun of her.

Worst of all, there would be lessons she wouldn't be able to recite and perhaps Teacher Chen would regard her as a wild child and would shake her head.

Dad very soon realized what was happening, he knit his brows and worked out when Aroma could go back to school. Aroma said that she was very independent and that they could wait until everybody had forgotten about it and then think again.

"A whole day's passed, that's twenty-four hours. They will have forgotten already."

"No, no they won't," wept Aroma bitterly, "they remember everything."

Dad did not force Aroma to go back to school and was particularly nice to her for those few days. He often brought back other flowers and planted them on the borders of the little flower country. Worried that she was unhappy, he believed that looking at flowers would cheer her up.

Duidui came every evening to help her with homework and Aroma dragged her to the sunflower and tried singing to it several times but it was still no good.

"Perhaps it's tired," said Aroma, embarrassed, "like people, sunflowers can't go on dancing all the time."

On Saturday, a doctor called Uncle Bag who worked with Duidui's mum at the hospital came to see Duidui's grandfather, bringing a physiotherapist with him to treat his twisted neck.

Uncle Bag unintentionally overheard the discussion about Aroma and made a point of telling Aroma's dad that there actually were certain plants that would dance to the sound of music. It seemed that the movement of auxin within the plant caused a change in the rate of cell growth. It was also possible that it was photosynthesis, or that certain plants were simply music lovers by nature.

"I say," said Aroma's dad in delight, "my daughter's the princess of the little garden country and that's why only she can see that wonderful sight."

Aroma was excited and breathed a sigh of relief. In her little head not every plant wanted to dance. There were some that couldn't and some that didn't have the courage. The world would be even more beautiful if there were more plants that could dance. Later, if there were children who saw sunflowers dance again, everybody would believe it.

Things seemed to take a turn for the better. But Little Ox wouldn't accept it. He came with Duidui and sang round the sunflower. He sang as brightly as a bugle and he particularly felt that a song should be sung loudly before it could be reckoned any kind of a song at all.

But the sunflower couldn't stand his singing and that round, round disc drooped downwards, even less willing to dance.

Little Ox believed that he had won and said, "Well, there's your big boast blown apart."

Aroma thought she would have a fight with Little Ox.

Duidui was very embarrassed. She hadn't seen the sunflower dance and hadn't been able to help Aroma. She stood in the way of Little Ox and asked Aroma, "When will you be back at school?"

"Not now, later, I want to wait until everybody has forgotten," said Aroma.

"But Teacher Chen says that if you go on playing truant you'll be put back a year."

Aroma said nothing. She felt that nobody cared about her and that she might just as well be a bad child.

"Please, come to school. You're the only friend I have. I don't get on with my desk-mate ... you know that." Duidui was somebody with sadness in her eyes but competitive as well. She liked to compete with the best girls in the class and when comparing height she would secretly stand on tiptoe.

"But ... I want to go when they won't mention it again."

Duidui's eyes reddened. She was strange. When she thought of something sad she immediately burst into tears, "Don't argue with Little Ox and the others about the sunflower dancing."

"I tell you. The sunflower I planted really does dance," said Aroma. "That's it. I hope everybody forgets it because perhaps it won't want to dance again."

Duidui gently shook her head and said, "I would really like to see it with my own eyes but, since you'd like me to forget, I'll forget absolutely everything."

"Really? Can you?"

"Yes."

"Then you'll completely forget who I am and we'll have to get to know each other again," said Aroma.

Duidui nodded and said, "Hallo, I'm Duidui."

"I'm Aroma."

"I know," she said, "your little brother is in the top class of our school's kindergarten. When he says your name it's like a mountain song."

Aroma said, "That's deliberate. He would like me to go and stop his mouth."

Duidui invited Aroma home. Aroma followed her pretending that she did not know the way and had forgotten everything and that it was all very funny and as if they had just met. Duidui and her family occupied the whole of the second floor, which had polished wooden floors and full-length metal windows.

They were the most well-off and best-housed family in all of Springwater Lane.

A Taste of Being Despised

Aroma had been to Duidui's home before. The reception room by the entrance had a bronze mirror and ornamental stools and old fashioned upright carved chairs. In Duidui's mother and father's room there was a jewel chest and a hair bucket, and a big bed, said to be really up-market, its frame made from ox bone inlaid with pear wood decorated with a carved pattern of nine lions and two phoenixes.

When Aroma used to visit Duidui's home she always chose a time when Duidui's grandfather was out. Duidui's grandfather was head of the household and was called Wu Dehua, but everybody in the building called him Elder Brother Ah De. This name was better known than his proper name.

None of the children liked the old man. He spoke fiercely and liked to shout, and he often had a stiff neck because his pillow had slipped during the night. It was hard to describe the look in his eyes as he gazed at you. It was as if his expression might produce an electric current, his stare causing wave upon wave of numbness in your scalp.

Besides, he was mean. The previous New Year, all the families of Springwater Lane had given sweets to their neighboring children. Duidui's grandfather had given least of all, a few old pine nut rice balls about to fall to bits for each child. He was even pleased with his own generosity, urging the children to repay him when they had grown up. He was wrapped in his own pride and had no sense of the children's feelings. Nor did he care what other people thought of him.

After that, the children all slipped away when he appeared, leaving just Duidui, who dared not disobey her grandfather.

Duidui's granny said that Duidui's grandfather had not been like that when he was young. He had not been so terrible and his neck had not been stiff. Everything had changed after Dr. Bag had removed a tumor that had appeared in his armpit.

Aroma liked to listen to Duidui's granny talking. She was very good-looking and wore smart black clothes, she was neat-handed and spoke softly.

She was doing embroidery when Aroma and Duidui came in. The embroidery table was huge and had a drawer as big as the top of the table.

Duidui greeted her with "Granny" and Aroma called her "Duidui's granny."

She responded and after putting away the embroidery rose and kissed Duidui on the cheek, saying, "This little peach mouth is charming." But she pronounced "peach" as "perch." She stroked Aroma's head and said, "Duidui is always happy when you come, she likes you a lot. I'll get you both something nice to eat in a moment."

There was a big screen in the reception room which divided it in half, leaving just a narrow opening to get through so that Aroma had never been to the half of the room on the other side of the screen. Seeing Aroma glance towards the screen Duidui said, "Aroma, what shall we play today?"

The big empty reception room had a romantic air. Aroma stretched out on tiptoe and traced a circle on the floor, saying, "I think I'd like to dance and fly round in circles."

"We'll dance ballet together," said Duidui happily.

"We'll dance the sunflower's dance to the sun."

Duidui's granny brought Aroma a sweet bean pastry and sent Duidui out of the reception room for a moment. Watching Duidi leave she jabbed Aroma with her elbow and whispered, "Remember, don't go looking at the screen."

"What's the matter?"

"Duidui'll be back in a moment," she consoled Aroma. "It's nothing, I'm here."

Aroma was a little nervous after Duidui's granny left. She deliberately didn't look at the screen and went to look at another part of the reception room. Hanging on the wall was a large red and gold tablet carved in deep relief. Aroma could make out

"Three Visits to the Thatched Hut". Another bit was "Savior Zhao Yun," both stories from the *Romance of the Three Kingdoms*. There was a niche in the wall beside the plaque and Aroma opened it and saw a beautiful wooden box inside. She remembered that Duidui had said that it was a document box with her mother and father's birth horoscope in it. Duidui said that the horoscope was ordained by the fairies and said that her mother was the bright star of the family and that her dad could marry no one but her.

But Aroma was very inquisitive. How was it that fairies were in charge of marriage? And why didn't her mum and dad have a document box? Why had Duidui's granny warned her not to look at the screen?

Aroma was extraordinarily curious and wanted to get to the bottom of it. She twisted to take a look. The screen was very magnificent, taller than a person and the red lacquer frame reached nearly to the ceiling. In its center was a panel of soft, white satin Suzhou embroidery with wild animals: lions and tigers at the top, and a huge eagle with its wings outstretched in the middle.

Aroma looked up, carefully examined the eagle and suddenly discovered that its eye was blinking. Unable to help herself she shrieked, "Oh! The eagle, the eagle, it's going to eat me!"

Perhaps that terrified cry was really frightening. Duidui's granny rushed in, white-faced, and pulled Aroma away and scolded, "You wretched old man, what are you up to? You'll frighten the child out of her wits."

Then Aroma heard a huge bang and something fell heavily against them. It was Duidui's grandfather who lay sprawled like a great leather sack with his neck out and slightly twisted, and the embroidered eagle screen crushed beneath him.

As it happens, when Duidui's granny had asked Duidui and Aroma into the reception room, he had gone along a corridor round the back and hidden behind the screen, standing on a bench and peeping through the eye of the eagle to see whether Aroma, left on her own, would behave badly. The blinking eye that Aroma had seen was his. The eagle eye in the screen was a fretwork that

Duidui's granny had wanted to sew up, but he wouldn't allow it.

"How can you be so stupid, spying on a child?" grumbled Duidui's granny.

"Leave me alone. This girl won't go to school and tells lies as well. I wanted to see how she behaved. She's a friend of my granddaughter, I needed to check this out." Duidui's grandfather was in a rage and thundered at his wife. He also said she was stupid and brainless.

Duidui's granny was very dignified. She maintained her composure and didn't get angry when Duidui's grandfather criticized her. It seemed that she was used to it. She pulled him up and dusted off his clothes, just as if she were dealing with a child having a tantrum.

Aroma understood, the fact was that Duidui's grandfather despised truants. He felt that Aroma was not a good child.

Aroma suddenly realized that not going to school was a serious matter.

She didn't want to be treated differently or looked down on.

The Innocent Liar

Duidui pulled Aroma away into the corridor to do ballet. She had a great sense of fun and stood on tiptoe with her neck extended, little lips pursed, red faced and now and then holding a ballet pose in front of the mirror. She was very much in love with her ballet self.

She slowly came close to Aroma and said, "My granddad's going to ask you questions, do you realize? Nobody in the family is allowed to tell lies. Granny hasn't told Granddad a lie in her life and Dad would never dare lie to him. Granddad hates people lying. Granddad says that if Dad had lied when he was a child, he would have cut out his tongue with a pair of scissors."

"Why is he so terrible?"

"No reason, he likes it that way," said Duidui, "... please don't say anything to Granddad about the dancing sunflower."

"But that's true," said Aroma.

Duidui said hesitantly, "You ... me, you mustn't say anything ... why do people talk so much?"

Duidui's grandfather was already up on his feet and was calling her.

There was nothing upstanding about this man. He was small and wizened but his eyes were round as balls and black as lacquer. They glared like a tiger as he looked at you.

"You! Can you truthfully say to me that you consider yourself a good girl?" He looked at Aroma as he spoke, his eyes filled with a strange mysterious power, like a very old cat.

Aroma hesitated a moment and said, "I do."

"Your mother apart, who really is that other female in your family? Don't be afraid. I'm just trying to get things clear about what sort of people I live on top of, whose garden I share and who I can see from the window when they get up in the morning."

"There's Dad, Mum, my little brother whose got a baby radio ..."

In a burst of irritation he said, "That female, who carries bucket after bucket of water into the garden ..."

"You mean Auntie Mai. She's part of our family, she's like a sort of ... maid."

He turned his face and looked at Aroma and said slowly and distinctly, "Look at you mumbling away. I'm not to be lied to ... don't you deceive me, I hear that she and your mother address each other as sister."

"Yes," said Aroma.

"Little cheat," he said, "you'll be telling me that sunflowers can dance next."

Looking at him as he wheezed away Aroma recalled what Duidui had said about scissors and tongue and was scared to death.

Duidui said at once, "Granddad, Aroma has never deceived anyone. The sunflower she planted did dance."

"You know for a fact?"

"I know," said Duidiu, "I saw it, really."

"You're talking nonsense. I'm going to get the scissors ..." said Duidui's grandfather.

Aroma subconsciously sealed her mouth so as not to let her tongue out and it lay pressed numbly against her gums. She already had a premonition of terror.

"It's true, it's true, it's true," said Duidui in loud tones.

Aroma listened in amazement and without waiting for an explanation quickly dragged Duidui away.

They went to the little garden country once more to see the sunflower that wouldn't dance. Aroma was desolated. She had expended a great deal to prove that she hadn't lied but had caused all this trouble. She broke into a sweat on Duidui's account. She said, "Duidui, you shouldn't have said that because you didn't see it yourself."

"I was afraid that Granddad wouldn't allow me to be friends with you." Duidui twisted her little mouth into a pout and said unhappily, "now I'm the same as you, a child that has told a lie. But don't tell anybody else."

Aroma was even more upset. Even Duidui didn't believe everything she had seen and even Dr. Bag's confirmation was of no help. She wondered what could be done. Duidui had told a lie on her behalf. Aroma had believed that if there was one person on earth who would never deceive anybody it was Duidui. That fine expectation was now shattered.

In the course of time Aroma distributed the seeds from the dancing sunflower to a lot of people so that the whole world could have dancing sunflowers. But who was there who believed her? She didn't know about Mum, Dad, her little brother and Auntie Mai and her classmates. And how many of the people she didn't know believed that sunflowers could dance?

Aroma thought and thought with a vague empty sort of feeling. She dragged Duidui into the little garden and prayed to the sunflower to dance and let Duidui see it once, whatever else happened. She said, "Please dance. That way Duidui won't be regarded as a liar ..."

However, Duidui didn't think that way and said, "Never mind, I can be an innocent liar."

Aroma recalled Duidui's grandfather's eye blinking through the eye socket of the eagle. The world contained doubt, disbelief and suspicion as well as lies and deception, but she was not happy and said, "But I don't want to be a liar."

"Good," laughed Duidui, "we can both stop worrying. We shall never be deceived."

Wonderful Orange Peel Candy

Aroma promised to go to school but although she said the words aloud they were still just a whisper in her heart. It was not that she was unwilling to go to school. It was just that she felt rather uncomfortable about it. Nor did she know how she was going to explain the business of the dancing sunflower to her teacher and classmates. In addition, it would be embarrassing when people started talking about her not being at school for the last few days.

Aroma was worried about being cold-shouldered and about losing face. When she heard something unpleasant her heart trembled and her face became a veil of red.

Dad realized what was worrying Aroma but said nothing and, as if rewarding her, took her shopping and bought her some marshmallows and her favorite orange peel candy, small thumbnail sized sweets made from sticky rice flour: soft, sweet, sticky and delicious.

Afterwards he took her to a shop called "*Laohu* Literary" and bought her a very good writing brush with small beads hanging from its shaft. Dad said that the shop's owner had built his fortune on Huizhou ink but had later branched out into writing brushes and paper. The shop had been established many years ago and was very famous. Scholars all knew of it and so Aroma should know about it too.

Aroma said, "I know of it but can I remember its name as

Laohu (tiger)? Then I won't forget."

Dad allowed Aroma to keep some of the sweets to share with her classmates at school. If anybody asked her a question she didn't want to answer she could say, "Have an orange peel candy." If somebody said something that made her happy she could give them a marshmallow.

Mum came and hugged Aroma, and attached a butterfly bow to her braids. The bow was a deep blue, very pretty and simple and made of crepe. When she had tried it out to her satisfaction she took it off and folded it up, saying that she would put it on again the following day.

Auntie Mai normally combed Aroma's braids. Sometimes she combed them very well and sometimes they stuck up all over the place. In fact, how they were combed depended upon Auntie Mai's mood.

"Mum combs better than Auntie Mai," said Aroma.

"Not at all," said Mum. Auntie Mai had to comb once a day and sometimes when she was very busy she might be careless but Mum didn't often have the chance to do any combing and was usually in a good mood and would make careful preparations.

"Tomorrow morning, would you like your hair loose or in a calabash plait?"

Aroma was happy and at the same time a little sad. Seeing her mother and father looking so serious she realized how the business of not going to school had worried them.

Her little brother came over and said, "I want a marshmallow."

Auntie Mai pulled him aside and made him hide behind the door to eat it. She liked him the most and after she had breast fed him looked on him as her own child. She didn't like to see mother and father crowding round his sister and forgetting him. She was afraid that he would feel deprived.

In fact, Aroma knew that Mum and Dad didn't like the way Auntie Mai fussed over him like a mother hen and said that if he had been a girl it would have been all right, but it wasn't right for a boy to be brought up so fussily. Boys and girls should be brought up differently.

In the morning Aroma dressed prettily to go to school. Mum did her hair in a calabash plait that looked lovely in the mirror. Auntie Mai tucked the newly bought superior writing brush into her school bag so that all could see it.

Little Ox was the first person Aroma met. He was always the first into school and the last to leave, as if it was he who opened up the school. He was very rough and had pulled Aroma's plaits in the past—pulled them so hard that Aroma had ached and her little mouth had grimaced. He carried on happily and said that if her plaits spread skyward she would be able to fly.

But Little Ox was rather simple minded. He loved his elder brothers. His third elder brother was born in the year of the dragon. He said dragons were best and flew very high; he himself was born in the year of the horse and horses were best because they galloped fast; his eldest brother was born in the year of the tiger, and tigers were best because they were lordly; his second elder brother was born in the year of the pig and pigs were the best because they liked sleeping.

Little Ox despised his younger brother Runthead. Runthead was younger by a year and was in the top class of the school's kindergarten. He had been born in the year of the goat, but because he had been born in the winter he was weak and timid and sometimes peculiar by nature. But for external consumption Little Ox said that goats were best because they ate a lot of grass.

"What are you doing here?" asked Little Ox straight out. "Aren't you being kept back a year?"

Aroma really couldn't bear him but, remembering the point that Dad had made, merely said, "Have an orange peel candy."

Little Ox looked at Aroma in amazement and asked, "Are you really the Aroma that was?"

Aroma again said nothing beyond, "Have an orange peel candy."

Little Ox asked a string of questions as well as talking a lot of unpleasant nonsense. Later on he stopped, perhaps because he didn't want to hear Aroma saying, "Have an orange peel candy."

Besides, Hehuan and the others who saw Aroma so well turned-out all exclaimed and crowded round and asked where her writing brush had been bought and wanted to see the tip of the brush. Hehuan said, "My brush is not as good as that. It's for medium script, yours is for the fine script that calligraphy teachers use."

Duidui was amazed at how well Aroma's plait looked and asked, "That calabash plait looks really pretty but how's it done? I want my granny to learn how."

Aroma distributed marshmallows to all. They ate them happily and felt that Aroma's return to school was a good thing.

Later on, even Little Ox was unwilling to pursue the matter because the business of Aroma not coming to school was already in the past. She now came every day. He was not interested in raising matters that were no longer novel. He was a boy with a real sense of his own dignity.

A Story of the Beginning of Summer

On the eve of the day of the Beginning of Summer, Aroma's mum crocheted two egg nets for Aroma and her younger brother, Didi. One was mauve and the other was dark blue.

"Oh, gosh," called Aroma, "Mum can do needlework as well!"

"How do they look?" asked Mum proudly.

Aroma's mum was a professional woman and household handicraft was not one of her skills. It was no easy matter to have crocheted two egg nets and it lit up the eyes of those who knew her.

Aroma thought that her egg net was not very pretty—it was a bit big—but Mum had made it with her own hands, with such warmth, so Aroma said, "It's lovely, it's not all twisted and it has a base. That's it, I can use it to catch fish with after the festival."

Auntie Mai said, "There are songs that are still fresh after a hundred years. A child's love for its mother is like that."

After the day of the Beginning of Summer, Auntie Mai specially boiled two large goose eggs for them. The careful minded Auntie Mai had discovered that chicken eggs in an egg net made the net appear even larger and emptier. The sight of Aroma entering school with a large goose egg at her breast attracted everybody's attention.

During break, Didi cracked his goose egg and together with Runthead came rushing over from the kindergarten to find Aroma, saying, "I don't want a rotten egg round my neck."

Little Ox heard him and excitedly shouted, "Rotten egg, rotten egg, two rotten eggs," at the top of his voice.

Aroma gave Little Ox a look. She saw that Didi's egg was truly badly damaged, cracked all over and split open, and said to him, "Then, you'd better eat it."

"Good! A tasty goose egg to eat," said Didi craftily, in high good humor.

Then Runthead upped and said that, in fact, Didi hadn't wanted the egg net round his neck in the first place and wanted to eat the egg and had bounced it on the ground like a ball.

Aroma said, "You really are a greedy-mouth."

"Goose egg yolk is big and yummy," said Runthead enviously. "I ate one a long time ago."

Aroma saw that there was nothing dangling on Runthead's chest and knew that there were a lot of children in his family and that his mother, like a vixen with cubs, was run off her feet and in no mood to crotchet egg nets for the children. There was nothing out of the ordinary about that.

But Runthead was very sensitive and told Aroma in a whisper that he had had a duck egg in syrup for breakfast, a large one, but it was impossible to hang it in an egg net.

Little Ox had sharp ears and hearing him said, out of the blue, "It was a fart egg that you ate in a dream. There's not an egg to be had in your family today. My mum didn't remember that it was the Beginning of Summer today, why should she? We have eggs every day!"

Runthead blushed to the tips of his ears and with his long hair looked rather like a girl. How nice it would be if he were indeed a pretty little girl. Aroma could hug him all the time.

It was lesson time and Teacher Chen said, "From now on we shall be writing essays."

"Really?"

Aroma opened her eyes wide, feeling almost supernatural. Could she really, like her teacher, write the characters she knew down on paper as an essay?

Teacher Chen said, "The essays we write in year two are not the same as writing single sentences. We are going to write about the Beginning of Summer. Remember, you must write about the characteristics of the Beginning of Summer and nothing else."

Everybody set to at once, sneaking a look at each other's work, unsure how to write and uncertain what the "characteristics of the Beginning of Summer" actually were.

"Teacher Chen, can I write about laying eggs and goose egg nets?" asked Aroma. "I want to write about a lot of interesting things."

"You can't write a lot. That sort of essay gets too diffuse. You must write about just one interesting thing," said Teacher Chen. "Use a story as a basis to describe the characteristics of the Beginning of Summer."

But at this point Aroma had no idea how to start, and when she handed it in the first essay that she had ever written in her life contained just two sentences, "There is a big goose egg in the egg net that Mum crocheted, it's really interesting. The characteristics of the Beginning of Summer are writing a story and now it's finished."

A lot of her classmates were much the same. They had written a bit more or less, thinking that the teacher's demands were rather high and impossible to meet, and then handed in their homework.

Teacher Chen, however, was very meticulous and examined the essays one by one. She looked at Aroma's with dissatisfaction, handed back the exercise book and said, "What's this about? It's the same as talking, do it again."

It was only Duidui's essay that Teacher Chen thought would do, and so she read it out.

Duidui's essay described how her parents and grandparents had vied with each other to make Beginning of Summer egg nets for her, but she loved her granny most of all and so on this morning of the day of the Beginning of Summer she had worn the egg net that her granny had made for her. Next year she intended to wear the egg net that her father had made for her.

Teacher Chen read out Duidui's essay and praised her, saying, "She wrote lots about the Beginning of Summer and knew how to capture its characteristics in her essay."

Teacher Chen also gave Duidui a good mark, patted her head and said that she had a very happy family.

Aroma was delighted because Duidui was her close friend and she was happy for her. Duidui's essay was well written and described how her whole family had made egg nets for her. But Aroma had not met with anything like this before. She still couldn't write about it and so just wrote, "The Beginning of Summer arrived, the Beginning of Summer came, the Beginning of Summer was fun, the Beginning of Summer left, the Beginning of Summer will come again next year, the Beginning of Summer ..."

She herself didn't know what to write about. She could only do the same as Duidui and in her second essay wrote the characters "Beginning of Summer" a number of times. As a result Teacher Chen did not return her essay.

"That's all right then," breathed Aroma in relief, "but I never want to write another essay."

Duidui's Pretty Mother

After school Hehuan came over and asked Duidui, "What sort of egg net did your father make for you?"

Duidui pouted and whispered, "I'm not telling you."

"Give me a look?"

"It should be like a stocking," laughed Duidui.

"Don't you see?" said Hehuan, "I want to look because my

dad never does sewing, he says it's women's work."

"My dad doesn't sew either," said Duidui angrily.

Duidui was not at all pleased. She told Aroma that she was determined to be the neatest, most outstanding and hardworking child ever and so her essay had described her family situation as the best possible. She believed that in the future it could really be as good as this.

"You described what you dream of, not what really is?" said Aroma.

Duidui's skin was very white and it seemed as if there was a network of blue buried within it. She heard what Aroma said and replied, "Yes, but I don't want Hehuan to know."

Duidui was the apple of her family's eye and it was said that her mother and father had been married for many years before she was born.

Duidui liked her father most of all. He was not the same as other fathers. He was big and tall, very whiskery and looked a bit of a rogue, but in fact he was soft-hearted and was always polite to both strangers and neighbors. It was said that he had been educated in Shanghai and he was fond of stamp collecting. Sometimes he would dry stamps on glass and he would stand there on guard as if gazing at a peep show. He was rather child-like and had a tin frog on a spring. When he was drunk he would say, "That frog can run."

Duidui looked like her mother but was often dissatisfied with her, saying, "My mother didn't make me an egg net. Only my granny boiled me some pigeons' eggs and dyed them. They looked like gold eggs."

"Perhaps she forgot," said Aroma. "She has a lot to remember at the hospital and has to remember the names of a lot of medicines as well."

"No way. When I mentioned it to her yesterday she said I was a grown child and didn't need an egg net."

Aroma said, "She's very busy you know, I haven't seen her for a long time."

"My mum's not as good as yours," complained Duidui. She

felt that she didn't have her mother's love and thus never felt the true warmth of a family.

Duidui said that it was her granny and granddad that had wanted her. Her mother hadn't wanted to have children. Her granny hadn't wanted to force her and could only gently wear her down. At the same time her mum always did what her granny said and so eventually had a child. Her granddad still wanted a grandson but it was no good, her mum was not prepared to have another. Her granny said never mind, so whatever her granddad said, her mum wouldn't listen. She was not prepared to have a son and had to treasure Duidui instead.

Just then, Duidui shouted, "Aroma, quick, come and look."

Aroma saw a child chasing Didi with his fist raised in anger and hitting him. Didi was scuttling away like a guilty rat shouting something as he escaped.

The child spat in the direction of Didi's back and soon seemed ready to resume pursuit.

Aroma rushed across with Duidui to help. They stopped the child and said, "Please don't hit people."

Didi, seeing that there was now no danger, shouted, "Bum, bum, bag bum."

The boy pushed aside the two girls and resumed his pursuit of Didi, who, seeing that there was no escape, dashed into the hospital next door to the school as the boy chased him.

Once in the hospital it seemed as if they had disappeared. They couldn't be found.

"That's my mother's hospital," said Duidui. "I know the way."

They rushed into Duidui's mum's hospital. They pressed the lift buttons for all floors for no other reason than that they wanted to find Didi. They searched around but didn't see Didi or the boy.

On the point of tears, Aroma said, "They're bound to be fighting somewhere."

"We'll find my mum and ask her to help," said Duidui.

They found Duidui's mum in the nurses' room. Duidui's mum was buxom and good looking. She had a high nose, a small but prominent mouth and clean tidy hair. She was a nurse and wore a white coat in the hospital but her ordinary clothes were very fashionable, and the heavy jewelry she wore was often changed. In addition, she liked buying pretty clothes for Duidui and dressed her like a doll. Duidui's mother was good in all respects but she often seemed very absentminded and sometimes bumped into people in the street.

Duidui told her mother everything and she said, "Ah, I know what we need to do."

She took them to Dr. Bag's office where they saw at once the boy and Didi standing side by side. The boy had very soon caught Didi.

Dr. Bag was telling them off. He was a surgeon from Shaanxi and looked like one of the terracotta warriors. The ridges of his face and the bits that stuck out or caved in were rather different from other people. So was the way he spoke: his tongue was big and it wasn't that easy to follow his accent.

As the two of them listened, they heard that that the boy was called Bag Bigu and was Dr. Bag's adopted son. Didi didn't know where he had heard that he was called Bag Pigu (Bag Bum) and had killed himself laughing. He always called him by that name and so had been chased and hit.

"Your problem is that you don't know each other," said Dr. Bag. "If you did and he called you Bag Bum, you could call him Bum Bag. You wouldn't feel that your self-respect had been injured. So, introduce yourselves."

"Bag Bum."

"Bum Bag."

Bag Bigu and Didi came to an understanding and became friends but Bag Bigu would have nothing to do with Aroma and Duidui and said, glaring at them angrily, "Huh, they think I'm easily put upon. Just wait and see."

It was said that Bag Bigu was short of words but long in self-respect. He had grown up in an orphanage but had escaped to join a circus where his master had disciplined him violently. Dr. Bag was a distant relative and Bag Bigu was already much better when the doctor took him in. But he had a strange fault: if somebody said something to him and it didn't happen, he considered him a fraud. He also took against anybody who didn't show him respect.

When Aroma heard this from Duidui she was rather nervous and asked Duidui's pretty mother what she should do. She said, "Don't bother about things that are already in the past, forget them. Most of the time people frighten themselves."

Subsequently, every time Aroma passed the hospital and saw Bag Bigu he took off at speed. It seemed that the boy trembled at the sight of her. It wasn't that he didn't know her but that he was afraid that she might stop him again. Consequently, she had no further worries.

However, Aroma did remember Duidui's pretty mother's reply.

Later, when Aroma visited Duidui's home she paid particular attention to Duidui's mother's lifestyle. Aroma's mother was aware of this and said, "Aroma, you should make more friends of your own age."

Perhaps Aroma's mother had heard something. She always disapproved of any closeness between Aroma and Duidui's mother. However, the persistence of the young does not follow the will of adults. It has a very clear aim: to imitate life, to copy people and to model a multitude of experiences that the young do not yet even know of themselves.

One evening when Aroma was playing at Duidu's home she saw Duidui's mum standing on the balcony gazing longingly at the sky.

Aroma asked, "Are you looking for the Big Dipper? You can only see it at night."

"I'm looking at a river in the sky," she said.

Aroma saw it as well. There was a rarely seen long cloud that lay horizontally across the sky, gleaming with a silvery light. She said, "It's really like a river."

"There was a great river at home and when I was young I really wanted to cross it and to see everything on the other side."

"But now you're on the other side."

"But when you reach the other side, what you see is still much the same. People are chasing the same rainbow."

Looking at Duidui's mum's grief-stricken expression, Aroma realized that what she was looking at was a river that broke the heart.

Smooth Tongued Didi

A tranquil joy returned to Aroma's life, nobody bothered her and she could look after herself.

In the evening, Aroma attended to the sunflower, watered it and dug the soil round it. Even if it wouldn't dance Aroma had no intention of letting it forget the rhythm of music.

Duidui liked to stand high on the second floor balcony and gaze through half-closed eyes on the scene below. She said that she envisaged the path below as flowing water and Aroma's little garden as a pool and the sunflower that had once danced was a strange kind of grass.

"Then, what am I?" asked Aroma, looking up.

"You're me, I've made you me."

Aroma picked up the cat, Snow White, and said, "And now?"

"I've changed into Snow White, being held like a baby, it's really comfortable."

The little white cat had come home from the market with Auntie Mai a month earlier. It had been the day of one of the traditional solar calendar divisions and Auntie Mai, who came from the country, was very observant of these days. She took festival days such as Tomb Sweeping Day in April and Bearded Grain in June and the Winter Solstice very seriously.

"These festival days were ordained by the Lord of Heaven," she said.

On that particular day, Auntie Mai carried a new linen handkerchief bordered with lotus flowers and was wearing a pair of embroidered slippers that Duidui's mother had given her. They were new and they were beautiful. She was worried in case some ill-mannered male deliberately trod on them and so intentionally walked one foot in front of the other, mincingly in and out, when a kitten suddenly appeared by her foot like a rolling ball and lightly scratched at the embroidered white orchids on her slippers. No one knew where it came from. The kitten did not know Auntie Mai and did not know that it was people's feet that were moving along the street, but somehow it managed to find the finest "fish" amongst all those feet. It took that unusual pair of embroidered slippers for its mother.

The kitten looked rather like a rabbit with thick fur and a short tail, its skin and hair were as white as snow but its ears were rather small and its mouth looked a little like that of a rabbit but not too obviously.

Auntie Mai kept the kitten and Didi gave it a name: Snow White.

Snow White loved dancing, but it was a circular dance, that went round and round as it tried to catch its own tail.

Taking advantage of Snow White's circular dance, Aroma immediately played the radio to the sunflower because the music being broadcast sounded like a dance tune that could accompany dance steps. However, the music had been playing for just a little while when trouble arrived.

Her younger brother Didi charged clumsily over. He wasn't alone either. There was another child with him, the youngest of Little Ox's brothers, commonly known as Runthead because he was last in line of the family.

Didi and Runthead had always been the best of friends and were playing together. All that could be seen was that they both had an arm around the other's waist, with the hands of their other arms all twisted up and trembling, as if their wrists had been broken. In addition, they had the common use of two legs, advancing as if three-legged and hitting the ground with a kind of skip. It was as if one had a bad right leg and the other a bad left leg, with the two bad legs dragging along as if they had rickets.

They were shouting, "Out of the way! Disabled hand and foot coming."

Of course, it was all made up. Their hands and legs were as nimble as anybody else's and Runthead was an accomplished high-jumper who could leap like a mountain rabbit. Nevertheless, the pitiful sight they presented was even more realistic than the real thing.

Aroma said angrily, "Two clumsy idiots in collusion."

"No we're not, we're one-armed, one-legged heroes," said Runthead.

Runthead had five brothers in all. His handsome eldest brother, Little Tiger, was a smart young man with long legs as slender as bamboo. He was also very polite and had gained entry to a well-known university. He was the most valued member of the family.

Mother Sui who ran the hot water shop once said that all the boys of the He family were handsome.

Aroma was not of the same mind. She thought that Little Ox had a mouth like a hippopotamus. She hadn't paid much attention to the others and although Runthead was quite good-looking with his sharp chin and bright eyes, he appeared too delicately built for a man. The strange thing was that if he allowed his hair to grow and washed his face a bit more, he would look just like a pretty little girl.

Runthead was dressed like a pauper child. He normally wore his next elder brother's hand-me-downs, either too large or too small and odd in style, but he always liked to be clean.

Not like Didi whose face at the moment was covered in mud, where from nobody knew. In the excitement of playing he hadn't paid attention.

Auntie Mai chased after him with a cloth saying, "You've only got one face and it must be kept clean. What a performance."

Didi escaped without trace.

When unable to find Didi, Runthead was disconsolate. On his own he didn't like having anything to do with other people and even walked with his head lowered. When he met people he knew he immediately made off elsewhere, kicking a tin as he went, not wanting to greet them.

Didi reappeared in a moment and Runthead cheered up. Once he had found Didi he became a happy child once more. He followed him around like his little shadow.

With great enthusiasm, laughing uproariously, they played a game of the film *The Rogue Prince* and then heard Little Ox shouting loudly.

Runthead turned and scampered off home. He was very aware of family customs. His "Foxy Dad" had not taught these to him. Foxy Dad liked talking too much and Foxy Mum loved her children dearly, and neither had taught their sons "manners" so they had grown up by themselves. Except that Runthead had four elder brothers and each and every one of them seemed to discipline his "little devil," particularly Little Ox who wielded absolute power over Runthead but was in absolute thrall to the other three.

Didi came over with a pathetic look on his face. He wanted to carry off the radio that Aroma was holding in order to listen to the folk music program, but in his haste didn't bother to speak properly and just took it, saying, "Give it to me, elder sister."

Aroma let him have it. She had never known how to refuse him. Didi worshipped her a little and often kept a wary eye on her as he went about his business. If she said "no" he would look at her in puzzlement, unable to think through why it was like this.

Aroma remembered very well what Auntie Mai had said about younger brothers and elder sisters. She had said, "Aroma, you need to treat your younger brother better. You must be good to all the family. If you kick the family dog, others get kicked as well. People will only take a family really seriously if there is mutual respect within that family."

Didi's love of listening to the radio was well known. Auntie Mai said that he had been like this in his cradle. When the radio broadcast a comedy duologue his two little hands would drum furiously in front of him as if beating in time with the words and music.

Later, the baby's odd behavior frightened Auntie Mai who simply turned the radio off. This made matters even worse. The baby turned and fell from its cradle hitting its head on the floor. At the hospital no symptoms of concussion were detected but there seemed to have been some injury and thereafter the child's temperament was not quite the same.

Didi liked listening to comedy duologues and listened as if in a world of his own. He also liked folk theatre comic dialogue and storytelling, his ear glued to the radio's speaker waiting for the faint sounds of the program's introductory music, as if longing for the return of friends who had been scattered afar.

The speaker of the duologue being broadcast at that moment had a northern Jiangsu accent and when talking in dialect deliberately exaggerated it so that "snow white shoes" became "snore wet seas." Didi thought this was fantastic. He particularly liked the off-key bits of the monologue and learned them one by one. The parts he couldn't get quite right he still learnt and the ones he could he performed glibly and smoothly.

When he heard that the somebody with sparse hair in the monologue was called Comrade Baldtop, he collapsed on to the bed rolling about laughing and thumping the wall like a madman.

Mum and Dad stood watching with flustered expressions, secretly exchanging glances and tapping their temples, indicating that there was something not quite right with this child.

Auntie Mai was grim-faced and upset. She protected Didi in all things and let nothing slip. She beckoned Aroma over and whispered in her ear, "Quick, tell Didi to stop, he'll listen to you. I really can't stand it. Why must your parents look like that? They should take more responsibility for their own son."

When Aroma went to him it so happened that Didi had just finished listening to a passage of monologue and was waiting with his thin neck outstretched.

Aroma went over to take the radio saying, "I'd like to listen to some music."

Didi turned away and said, "Don't steal my precious treasure from me, sister. Don't be a robber."

Aroma said nothing and looked at him severely so that Didi could only say, "I'll let you have it to listen to music for a little while."

The radio started broadcasting music.

"This music's no good, it's like the wind whistling," said Didi.

Aroma said, "The whistling of wind makes good listening. In the music the wind has a color. Now it's green."

But Didi saw it differently. One moment he said the wind was blue and the next he said it was yellow.

Later, he took advantage of Aroma's inattention, grabbed back the radio, escaped through the window and climbed into the magnolia tree where he sat in the fork of a branch listening to a sing-song duologue performance of *A Visit to the Great World*, an amusement park in pre-war Shanghai. He sat there confidently, pulling other branches across and wrapping them around himself. People passing underneath were sometimes startled by the strange sound of laughter that now and then emerged from the midst of the tree's leaves. Occasionally, broken twigs would also fall.

A Parent's Heart

Aroma's mother and father were still worried and wanted to "test" Didi.

The next day, in the evening, Didi again seemed to want to get inside the radio and whilst listening to a monologue called *The Son-in-Law* burst out laughing at a particularly funny passage.

Dad was home from work, saw him and said, "Just look at him, laughing like an idiot."

Mum said, "It really makes you worry."

The radio program continued broadcasting with no sign of stopping when suddenly the electricity failed. It was as black as pitch and there was not a sound to be heard.

Didi was utterly at a loss and could not express his anger. He deliberately stood in the middle of the room shouting and screaming, "I'm scared, I'm scared!" as well as saying, "I'm lost, I'm lost," a number of times. He didn't know what it was all about, but anybody could see that Didi was doing something extremely odd.

Mum rushed in and took him aside to play, without noise and peacefully. Didi was not at all happy and kept on saying, "For heaven's sake," indicating astonishment and resistance, quite deliberately on his part.

"Are you so upset because you can't listen to monologues? Are you no longer Didi without them?" asked Dad angrily.

"Why is it, why is it," Didi asked, "that other houses have light but we don't?"

Just then there was the sound of a voice: "Is anyone at home?"

"Are you the electrician?" Didi rushed out and asked.

"No, I've come to look for my cat."

"Don't come here," said Didi. "Be off with you!"

Dad silenced Didi with a shout and quickly went and thumped the meter box. He fiddled familiarly around and the electricity was immediately re-connected.

Didi rushed off to the little room.

This unexpected guest had been looking for his cat everywhere and hearing that a cat had been picked up here had rushed over to have a look.

Dad bent down and looked everywhere, thinking to bring Snow White out.

"Gone missing," announced Didi, "can't be found, Comrade Baldhead."

"Didi!" said Dad severely.

The childish younger brother continued glibly in the same tone. Because Auntie Mai spoilt him so, at the age of seven he still couldn't spit out the bones when eating fish. Auntie Mai had raised him from when he was small. When she was around there was nothing that he dare not do.

Having not seen the cat the caller was reluctant to leave, "Gone missing? Gone with whom?"

After he left everybody went to bed. Aroma went to the wardrobe to fetch her pajamas and suddenly, hearing a *xixi susu* sound from inside, said, "There's a mouse!"

Dad opened the door to discover that Didi had hidden Snow White in the coat cupboard where it had fallen asleep. It now opened its mouth wide and emitted an immense yawn.

Dad wanted to take Snow White to the home of the caller. Didi was unwilling and made a great fuss. He still believed that everybody was there to do his bidding and his two little hands tore at his father's clothes without letting go.

"It's somebody else's cat and should go home," said Dad. "The gentleman left me his address."

Didi was so distressed that he was confused. He waved his hands as if brushing something away and suddenly said in the glibly humorous style of a monologue, "Why you come pickin' a fight with me then?"

Dad was so enraged that he slapped him and said that Didi would never be allowed to listen to those programs again.

Didi, shouting and yelling, unwilling to admit that he was wrong and with a tear-stained face, charged across to have it out with his father. Dad was about to teach him a lesson, raised his hand and then lowered it because Auntie Mai, hidden somewhere far away, had started to cry. Whenever Didi wept she felt that a piece of her heart had broken away and so Dad didn't have the heart. He was so careful of the little sprouts and insects in the garden that he didn't like to raise his hand to hurt anyone.

Didi cried for a while as if heaven and earth had been split asunder. Dad waited. He believed that when a child was angry or hurt it was best to let it all out.

When Didi's crying was its worst he clutched his head and rolled about on the ground like the Monkey King under the spell of the monk Xuangzang.

Auntie Mai hurriedly led him away to another room and made him lie down and fetched hot water infused with Chinese medicine and bathed his head in it. People said that where she came from it was a local form of hydrotherapy.

Aroma crept quietly over to see him. She was rather worried. The back of Didi's head was still in the warm water and he looked quite weak with his hair floating there like waterweed.

Didi faked a smile when he saw Aroma, he couldn't manage a real one.

"Get better soon," Aroma said.

"Dad didn't take away the radio, did he?" asked Didi. "What about Snow White?"

Aroma stealthily brought him the radio and Snow White as well. He hugged the cat to himself and let it listen to the radio. He switched on and turned the sound right down and with his ear pressed against it a smile appeared on his face and his lips smacked in appreciation.

"I'll soon be better."

He listened for a bit and performed a passage from *Congratulations, Sir* for Aroma in which he played both comic parts. At the end he said, "You didn't laugh."

Aroma didn't laugh and he did another extract from *Satisfied or Not?* in a strange accent more overdone than the movements. More than anything he liked to get people to laugh with his exaggerated performance.

Aroma laughed. She knew that if she did Didi would attempt to make her laugh next time as well, hoping that the fun would continue. If she kept a straight face throughout he would be disappointed and, as if his self-respect had been damaged, would not come to try and make her laugh for a long time. Downcast and like a bird with sodden feathers he would avoid her.

The next day Dad sent a polite message by his son to the caller and as a result he came to collect Snow White straightaway. He looked at the cat carefully, shook his head and said that it was not his family's cat.

Dad said, "Didi, I knew this early on. There was no need for all that fuss yesterday. Everything that happens in the world happens, it can't be avoided, all you can do is face up to it properly."

Didi who had been miserably hidden away in his room was so delighted that he rushed out with both arms raised.

Aroma loved the bright-eyed Didi she saw then and hoped that his happiness would continue.

The Miser's Banquet

From outside the alley came the voice of the seller of fried Ginko nuts: "Wang Ahda's fried ginko nuts, piping hot to touch, delicious to taste. Buy a bag for your son ... if you don't have a son buy one for your daughter." His voice was rather hoarse with a tinge of supplication to it. He spoke with a local Pudong accent so that "piping hot" became "bibing tot" and "delicious to taste" became "malicious to waste." This was followed by a long drawn out breath that softened the heart.

"Auntie Mai, I want to buy one," said Aroma.

"Buy two, I want one as well," responded Didi. "I still want something else."

Auntie Mai pretended to look shocked, her teeth protruding a little. She had always been a little buck-toothed though it didn't show when her mouth was closed, when it just bulged a little as if there was something rather good hidden inside. Consequently, her mouth was closed more often than not.

Auntie Mai combed her hair with a shiny comb. Her hair was coiled in a bun, the front hair and braids were long and thick and the hair was luxuriant enough to share with several people. Before she set to work she always tied up her braids and fixed them on her head with several long black clips that looked like centipedes. Otherwise she couldn't get going.

"They're ten cents a bag," she whispered. "It's like eating money. If I use all of today's market money, it'll just be rice for supper."

"You've got lots of market money left over," said Aroma.

Auntie Mai controlled the family finances. At the beginning of each month she got Aroma to help her divide that month's market money into thirty lots and pack it into thirty separate packets. She only took out one packet a day which she spent carefully and economically. Any money left over was saved and another packet used the following day and so on until the end of the month when she would prepare a sumptuous feast for the whole family. The family called this monthly banquet "the miser's revenge." Didi was said to have produced this name off the top of his head. The family thought it was funny and followed his lead. Later everybody used the name. Any outsider hearing it would certainly have thought it extremely odd, but outsiders never did hear it.

"We can just have fried rice without any vegetables tonight," said Aroma.

Didi said, "If you add a little scallion to fried rice it's delicious. Scallion is a vegetable."

"No nourishment," said Auntie Mai, "your father won't agree."

"We like it," they both protested, "fried rice, fried rice, we want fried rice."

"Very well, you shall have fried rice but don't think to get anything else ..."

Auntie Mai went and bought one bag of gingko nuts for them to eat between them. Once peeled they were a lustrous green, gleaming attractively like pearls, so that Aroma wanted to hold back and was reluctant to eat them. However, she found them a little bitter as did Didi and they just ate a few. In fact it wasn't that they wanted to eat the nuts, they just wanted to have them.

Everybody had fried rice for supper. Auntie Mai had added a little dressed salad that was fresh and appetizing and economical as well. After the rice, in a sort of conjuring trick, she brought in a Ningxia pudding: "sticky rice pieces." Several days earlier she had been seen soaking the glutinous rice. After steaming and pounding it she pressed it into a mold and then turned the mold out into a basket to dry in the sun. When it was ready to be eaten it was cut into slices and soya flour and sesame seeds were added. The steamed rice pieces were large, soft and sticky with the sesame seeds wrapped in the middle.

Sticky rice pieces were tougher than New Year rice cakes. Aroma and her brother stuck their chopsticks in and twisted them round vigorously before they could roll some round the chopsticks and then stretch it between them to dip in white sugar.

"If it were like this every day it would be wonderful," said Didi unctuously. "A crosstalk piece says eating must be appetizing and drinking must be hot."

Dad said, "What's that? It's 'eat fragrantly and drink pungently.' You listen to crosstalk but can't remember it properly."

Mum said to Dad, "You'll have to speak to him again. He listens to crosstalk as if he would like to clamber inside the radio."

Dad said, "Listening has to produce some sort of thought in the mind. Just swallowing it whole is hopeless."

Auntie Mai said not a word about the two children having made a fuss about buying gingko nuts. Thereafter Aroma and Didi loved her even more because with her there was no need to pay so much attention to manners.

At the end of the month Auntie Mai once more prepared her banquet.

She announced that she would cook a little more casserole and there would be other things as well.

It was really exciting and the two children shouted, "The miser's banquet!"

Mum and Dad laughed knowingly.

Auntie Mai, pretending to be offended, said, "Master and mistress, just see how annoying these glib-tongued youngsters are. I don't know where they get it from."

Auntie Mai was busy on account of all this. Of course, she was usually busy anyhow but tried to do something new every day. However, she still did the things she often did and liked doing and she still seemed never to weary of the same daily rhythm.

On this point, Auntie Mai resembled Duidui's granny in some respects.

Auntie Mai was of the same temperament as Duidui's granny and had learned from her how to make many Ningxia sweets. She had also learned from her how to make casserole. She cut the meat into very small pieces and stewed it at a high temperature so that it was tender, and the color was neither white nor red. The shrimp soya sauce she used—not strong—she made herself. The meat stewed in its alcoholic flavor and the juices flowed. The meat was ready to serve when it was soft but not oily, with the skin slightly puckered.

Before the banquet Auntie Mai always said, "You two youngsters go and bath."

"But ..." Aroma and Didi both shouted, and it was always, "bath after we've eaten!"

Auntie Mai always deliberately strove for perfection in her "miser's banquets" as if it were a kind of ceremony. This evening she wished for everything to be as she wanted, a magnificent feast, good looking children all spick and span and an atmosphere of domestic harmony, and lights.

Auntie Mai did not give in and insisted that Aroma should go and bath at once, saying that the water was just hot enough, "Go and fetch the water, otherwise there'll be nothing to eat."

Aroma and her brother went to the garden to fetch the bath water, calling "Heigho, heigho," as they carried in the full pails of what Auntie Mai called "sun water." The whole family had to obey Auntie Mai.

Auntie Mai liked to put water under the sun to heat as "sun water." Aroma knew that Mum had specially bought several large wooden water buckets for Auntie Mai. Mum paid particular attention to what Auntie Mai said and called her "younger sister."

As long as it was a day when the sun was out, Auntie Mai would pour tap water into two wooden buckets and cover the top with a thin cloth tied at the side. She then put them in the sun in the corner of the garden, rushing out to shift them to follow the sun around. By sunset the water was warm.

Auntie Mai removed the cover from the pails and poured the water into two basins for the children to bath in. Auntie Mai loved water and when she poured it, it produced a beautiful liquid sound like rippling green waves that made the heart itch with joy. Aroma wanted to do the same but however she tried she could not manage to produce the same lovely sound.

Aroma asked Auntie Mai, "At home, was your house surrounded by lots of rivers?" Aroma recalled a little village of delicate water that she had seen in a film, where every house faced on to a stream. She really wished she could be inside that film.

Auntie Mai shook her head and said, "Who said that?"

"Well, when did you start liking water?"

"I was born in the year of the fish. Fish can't exist out of water," said Auntie Mai. "I often used to dream that I was swimming, looking for my child, but I haven't had that dream since I came here."

Aroma was one and a half when Auntie Mai arrived. When Didi was born and his mother hadn't enough milk herself, Auntie Mai had volunteered to breastfeed him and had become his wet nurse. She had cared for Didi and felt he was like a child that she had brought with her from her old home.

Auntie Mai was a young woman who had once been married and her first child had been a daughter called Pure Water. Her husband's family had lost face but had not made a fuss and had taken the child and looked after it, so that Pure Water had become one of their own and of no great concern to Auntie Mai. She became pregnant again and had given birth to another girl. Her husband's family said that she gave birth to "burdens of debt" and her wretched man had paid no attention. One day she had gone to hospital with a high fever and when she returned several days later, the child was not to be seen. She heard that her husband's family had sent it to distant relatives who lived in Shanghai.

Auntie Mai said, "That little child of mine was really pretty, like a picture on a new year card. I liked to put a tiger hat on her and kiss her little round face. When she was sent to Shanghai I moved here to find her. As for my husband's family, none of them should try to stop me."

Auntie Mai's story had been told many times. Everybody knew that after she had moved it had been discovered that the distant relatives had secretly moved to an undisclosed destination. As a result, she had come to Aroma's home as a domestic help while she sought news of her child.

During the family banquet, Didi ate away and thought of folk song programs. He went off to listen to *Choosing a Partner* and *Guan Zhong Battles Qin Qiong* and completely ruined the atmosphere round the table.

Mum very much disapproved of Didi listening to these programs, saying that to be so slippery in speech so young was a sign of unreliability. Dad believed that conversation round the table should be about pleasant topics and so did not intervene.

Everybody believed that it was a great joy to benefit from the delicacies of every day saving. It was a pleasure to think of today, and tomorrow would be fine. It was a happy day.

Happiness lasted because Aroma's family life consisted of today and then tomorrow and then forever.

Foxy Dad

Duidui came to play. She knew Aroma and Didi and Auntie Mai as well and so she came when she wanted without feeling awkward. She looked at the dining table. She knew that the delicacies that Auntie Mai prepared for the "miser's banquet" had all been learned from her grandmother but she still liked to look and verify it with a sense of pride.

Auntie Mai called Duidui "Young Lady" and secretly ridiculed the attention she paid to dress. There were times when Duidui burst through the door wearing a red hat, showing off a little, the very model of her mother, the nurse.

Auntie Mai made Duidui taste the casserole. Duidui shook her head. She didn't like meat, even more so when she was a guest, and just said, "We have it at home."

Then, not wanting to go she stood at the window playing at palm prints on the glass. She clenched her fist and pressed the heel of her plump palm against the glass producing a shape with a hollow to it. She then carefully added five toes and it became a baby's footprint.

Aroma joined her in playing palm prints.

Just then there was the sound of activity outside below. It seemed to be somebody saying, "Over here, idiot, over here."

In a hurry Aroma opened the window with a bang. She looked out and saw that it was Little Ox who had brought his younger brother Runthead with him. He had a spade in his hand and was about to dig up the sunflower and take it away.

"Runthead saw the sunflower dance. It can dance a very funny kind of dance," said Little Ox. "He saw it just now when it was getting dark."

"I've seen it I don't know how many times," said Aroma. "It's not strange at all, it's beautiful."

"Exactly, that's it, exactly," Didi said.

Little Ox said, "We've come tonight to dig it up and plant it at home so that it can dance for our Foxy Mum."

"No, you can't. No, you can't, it's my sunflower," said Aroma.

She leaped down from the window in a rush and Didi, holding the radio, followed her but fell down as he jumped. He clasped the radio tightly to him and made off like a puff of smoke.

Little Ox took not a bit of notice and said loftily to Aroma, "Do you know who planted the seeds under your window? It was me. This sunflower should bear the He family name."

"That child is a very stubborn one," said a flustered Auntie Mai. "You don't want to cross it otherwise, if it dies, you'll have to pay."

"See reason. You'd better not get in my way," said Little Ox rudely.

"So you've learned from those barbaric little devils elsewhere have you. How can you be so unruly?" asked Auntie Mai.

Just then there was the sound of wheezy coughing.

Runthead tugged at his elder brother's jacket and whispered, "Leave it. Foxy Dad is coming, let's go."

It was Little Ox's father. His surname was He and in the local dialect the "He" was pronounced "Hu" like the Hu which meant fox. He was a little older than the other fathers, quite thin with crooked eyes and a long narrow face. He looked a little like a fox and walked with one shoulder raised. Early on his wife had let the children call him "Foxy Dad" and through use it had later become his nickname. Everybody called him Foxy Dad and later they became used to calling his wife "Foxy Mum" as well.

Foxy Dad said, "Where's the peepshow? Little brother Didi is playing a joke on me."

What had happened was that Didi had run over and told Foxy Dad that Little Ox wanted him to come and see a peepshow.

Little Ox turned his fire on Didi, glaring at him fiercely, saying, "Just you wait, just you wait."

"Don't wait, don't wait, I've gone," interrupted Didi deliberately. He was a little afraid of Little Ox and always had been.

Little Ox was a very nasty child and particularly stubborn, Duidui's granny said that he was "implacable." If you don't know, that means that he's a kind of violent person, different from everybody else on earth, with the temperament of an ox who, once angered, will rage on forever.

His father, however, was not like this at all. Although his nickname was "Foxy," he was actually a very genial man, utterly unlike his nickname. Foxes should be cunning but to call him cunning would be to do him an injustice. He called all children "little brother" or "little sister."

However, perhaps he had been cunning in the past, thought Aroma, because people did not acquire a nickname for no reason at all. Sometimes the nickname represented the real person better than the ordinary name.

To tell the truth, Aroma didn't like people with ugly-sounding nicknames, because when you said them your mouth didn't feel too happy about it, as if you had said something horrid and vulgar. For example, there was a boy in class called "bum beetle" and another called "scab head" and some were called even worse: there was a boy called "forefather fart." In these circumstances, Aroma had to omit a word or two and just call him "forefather," or call them by their given names. Given names could be used without a problem. No father or mother would give their child a name that was ugly or vulgar.

"Little sister Aroma," said Foxy Dad, "has Little Ox been annoying you?"

Aroma said, "Foxy Dad, come and sort it out."

Foxy Dad said, "Right, little sister, I'll come and be the judge."

Aroma looked at his smiling face and thought that it was very homely to use the nickname Foxy Dad. Were it not for the fact that Little Ox wanted to pull up the sunflower it would be quite fun, the same as a children's story.

She said, "Then you must be the best judge of all."

"Ha, ha," Foxy Dad was amused as he listened to Aroma. He had no daughters of his own and so particularly liked girls.

At that moment Duidui's grandfather came over. He had heard somebody below saying "watch the peepshow" and had come to have a look. He was not on speaking terms with Little Ox's father. It wasn't that they were unacquainted but that they despised each other and did not get on. The two of them faced each other and Duidui's grandfather twisted his head away and without a greeting snorted "Huh" through his nose.

Grown-ups fighting? Their technique is the same as children's. Foxy Dad took no notice and didn't snort, adopting a superior air of "nothing to do with me." He just told Duidui to go home.

Little Ox said, "I sowed a lot of seeds there. They sprouted, they're mine."

Aroma said, "That's not fair, that's my little garden and the sunflower I planted."

Foxy Dad said, "Right, I'll be the judge. You two will share the sunflower. Little sister Aroma and Little Ox, come and draw lots."

"Share the sunflower?"

He prepared two lots. On one slip he wrote "Sunflower pot" and on the other "Root and leaves," then he said, "If either of you refuses to draw then it's divided into two. Now let's draw."

He cupped his hands over the two slips, closed them and let Aroma draw first.

Aroma shook her head with a downcast expression, most unwilling to draw. Little Ox, on the other hand, seized a slip opened it and said, "I've got the pot, that's a bargain, there are seeds in it and I can replant." So saying, he leapt forward to grab the pot.

"Slowly," said Foxy Dad, "now listen to the judge delivering judgment. I award this sunflower to little sister Aroma."

"What!" shouted Little Ox, "that's out of order."

"You just wanted the sunflower itself, you had no intention of cherishing it or of looking after it. Right, the sunflower goes to little sister Aroma and when the seeds are collected in the autumn she must remember to share half of them with you."

"Right, Foxy Dad," said Aroma with delight.

Little Ox exploded with fury, snatched the radio out of the hands of Didi and held it up high as if to smash it on his own head. Didi cried out, that radio was his lifeline. Foxy Dad and Auntie Mai rushed to prevent Little Ox and pushed him against the wall. Didi hastily snatched back his treasured radio. In a moment, Little Ox charged over again, grabbed hold of Didi and with a cry of "huzza" lifted Didi and his radio up high.

"You, you're defying me," said Foxy Dad.

"Put him down, put Didi down, it's dangerous," screeched Auntie Mai.

Little Ox, as if sleepwalking, circled round with Didi held high and was about to smash him against the wall.

Everybody stood aghast.

At that moment the radio crackled into sound and began to broadcast a comedy. Suddenly Didi bellowed, "Put me down at once! *The Musician from Ningpo* has started."

Then, as if nobody was there, he started to sing, "2, 4 ... 3, 5, 7, 1, 2 ... 4, 1 ..."

Little Ox stood dumbfounded for a moment and put Didi down. He later said that he had really been so angry that he felt as if he was holding up a huge stone and when the "huge stone" had begun to talk and sing he had been frightened out of his wits.

A Family Story

On Sundays, Aroma's mum visited her own mother and Auntie Mai got up particularly early to prepare presents for her to take home. Usually she cooked two meat and vegetable dishes. Sometimes they were dishes that her mother liked, like salted yellow croaker or stir-fried vegetables or stuffed winkles. Sometimes she steamed a tray of buns stuffed with strips of radish or baked buns filled with sweet bean paste. She felt that these presents were real, substantial and not a waste of money. They would also give Aroma's grandmother less to do and save on refreshments.

Auntie Mai was very loyal to Aroma's mum. She not only helped her manage the household and children, she was also a high-level adviser on life generally. It so happened that Aroma's mum was not good at housework or social relationships and thus with Auntie Mai it was a case of hear and obey. They also addressed each other as sister.

Nevertheless, Auntie Mai still referred to Aroma's parents as "sir" and "madam" and would never change. Moreover, she liked her employers to be busy elsewhere leaving her in control of the household and all its decisions.

When Aroma's mum went to see her mother, Aroma and Didi reckoned they would have their own friends over to play. Dad didn't stay and always found that there was some place that he absolutely had to visit and so went off to his factory.

Once her employers had left, Auntie Mai reigned supreme happily in the household and energetically mopped the floors and allowed the two children to get up a little later. She delighted in an environment rendered sparkling clean by her own hands, saying, "You can't get up until the floor is absolutely dry, otherwise little footprints will spoil it."

Little Ox's mother, Foxy Mum, appeared suddenly as if by magic. Her arms and legs were very soft and she had an unusual sense of smell that allowed her to detect whether Auntie Mai's employers were at home or not. If they were, there was no way that she would come swaggering in. She said that they were too cultured and she felt that cultured people were somehow peculiar and that she couldn't get to grips with their knowledge of the world.

"What to do? Little Ox just wouldn't give up, he mounted a sit-in protest in front of our bed in the middle of the night."

"What was he on about?"

"It was about his row with Foxy Dad last night. He says he twisted his arm and made him lose face."

"So that was it," said Auntie Mai.

"That child is a real worry, he has too much of a temper," said Foxy Mum, going on to complain, "he has the makings of a robber."

"Let it be. I think you are fondest of him, otherwise how could such a small child have such a nerve?"

Auntie Mai and Foxy Mum were close. Foxy Mum's social status was low and people gossiped about her behind her back. She took this to heart, she despised the contemptuous glances she received and was filled with resentment.

Despite her lack of financial skills, at the beginning of the month her family managed comfortably and dishes that Foxy Dad liked, such as bighead carp and pork steamed with rice flour, were often on the table. The pork steamed with rice flour was made from the fattiest pork ribs, large and thin with skin and gristle, and coated with rice flour mixed with seasoning. After being thoroughly steamed so that the meat expands, the strips of pork become transparent and the skin wrinkled. However, by the end of the month the family couldn't get by. Everything had been eaten and there was nothing left and they had to borrow money.

Foxy Mum didn't go to the people who spoke ill of her. She had no desire to see the looks on their faces or give them a pretext for gossip. When she borrowed money it was to Auntie Mai that she came. Auntie Mai always had some change about her and she also taught Foxy Mum about financial management.

Once together they were never lonely. Whispering together Auntie Mai first taught Foxy Mum to pickle eggs by adding some sorghum spirit so that the yolk yielded oil. Foxy Mum then began to discuss the extravagance of Brother Ah De's household.

Foxy Mum said, "Just now they were boiling Yangcheng lake crab meat for crab oil to eat with noodles. The whole house smelled of seafood, it made me die of hunger."

"I'll go and beg a bowlful from Brother Ah De for you."

Foxy Mum shook her head like a rattle and said, "That one!"

Auntie Mai and Foxy Mum were chatting away happily when Mother Sui bounded in saying, "I've come to prick up my ears and save you the bother of re-arranging my household."

Auntie Mai said, "Yes, we were just gossiping about you but alas, we couldn't think of anything nasty to say."

They enjoyed talking about people who weren't there: people at a distance could be discussed freely.

They also discussed the well-dressed Duidui's granny, who outwardly seemed rather stuck up but who actually enjoyed people and unlike her husband was kind and good-natured.

Eventually, Duidui's granny arrived as well. It was not often that the four of them were able to get together secretly and unseen by others. Foxy Mum and Duidui's granny were able to get on because they had both visited Xi'an and been on an airplane, but there was no such fellow feeling between the two husbands and that made them feel awkward. They had to maintain their husbands' dignity.

They never spoke to each other in public and in order to avoid embarrassment they sometimes pretended not to have seen each other.

Aroma didn't want to get up. She loved listening to Foxy Mum and the others' stories about the neighbors and so pricked up her ears and paid careful attention.

Foxy Mum said that when Foxy Dad was young he had met a girl who had moved him to passion and he had frittered away all the family property on her. But the chicken flew and the egg was broken: the girl had left and married the son of wealthy parents. Foxy Dad had been heartbroken and later when he had met a nice girl, that's to say Foxy Mum, she had taken pity on him and decided to marry him.

After Foxy Mum had left, Aroma interrupted to ask, "If a lady pities a gentleman does she marry him?"

"Who says so?"

"Foxy Mum did."

Auntie Mai said, "So she says, but she just liked him and gave up everything for him."

"But does Foxy Dad like her?"

"He must do, otherwise how could he have lived with her for so long?" Auntie Mai went on to say, "There are some songs that never tire. You could discuss relations between men and women for a hundred years and still not get them straight."

Aroma was not convinced. Auntie Mai's answer had contained both confirmation and denial.

Aroma felt that Foxy Mum was not the same as other women. She had seen the world, her skin was smooth and dark, she had an air of elegance and charming eyes but her jaw was out of shape: her lower jaw protruded a little and the upper jaw couldn't close over it.

Mother Sui had once said that this was called "earth embracing heaven."

When the cold weather arrived Foxy Mum wore a surgical mask when she went out. You couldn't confuse the season and she wore the mask until early spring and didn't take it off until the weather was too hot to bear.

While she was wearing the mask, Foxy Mum appeared a great beauty but after she took it off the defects of her jaw were apparent and her mouth was a little crooked when she smiled. Unless you looked carefully you might think that there was something wrong with it. Not only did earth embrace heaven, it wasn't straight. Auntie Mai had looked carefully and said that Foxy Mum was just petulant, there was nothing else wrong with her mouth.

But Foxy Mum was good-looking. Her skin was like an expensive fur, smooth and taut and glowing with an unusual light.

She very much wanted to be pretty and wore leather sandals like those worn by schoolgirls. She was warm towards people and talked a lot, her voice was often hoarse. There was a special kind of odor about her, not unpleasant yet not pleasant, rather heavy as if it belonged to her alone. When she arrived, the familiar scent that assailed the nostrils came with her and when she left it followed her out.

But Foxy Mum was good to her husband and called him Foxy Dad and looked after him well and always put the appetizing bits in his bowl with her chopsticks.

"He just has to think of something and she will do all she can to see that he gets it," said Auntie Mai. "Foxy Dad wanted a whole flock of children and she bore him five in quick succession and her body never lost its shape."

Aroma was stunned. Foxy Mum's kindness to her husband seemed everlasting. She had been willing to bear five children for him, to lead a poverty-stricken life, and to borrow money.

Auntie Mai said, "This was arranged by previous generations."

"Why did the previous generations make this arrangement and not some other?" Aroma asked Auntie Mai.

Aroma was fond of dreaming and fond of her father too because he was tall, kind and could guess what was on her mind. However he did not know her most secret thoughts. For example, Aroma would think: if Dad hadn't met Mum and had married somebody else then there might not have been a daughter like her. In that case, even if she had stood face to face with Dad he wouldn't have recognized her or known that she was called Aroma.

How hurtful that would have been, how sad.

Aroma felt a vague sadness welling up in her heart. She felt curious as well. Why was it that she had to think of this now and not before?

Fortunately Dad's bride had been Mum, that was good and something to be happy about.

Three Brothers Snap Chopsticks

Duidui came to play with Aroma. She liked to whisper secretly with her under the pomegranate and cherry trees that stood close together and which her grandfather had planted the year she was born.

"Just give Little Ox the sunflower," said Duidui. "I'm thinking of giving him my tree to look after as well. He's very good at it."

Duidui was sometimes naive and sometimes knowing. She felt that Little Ox had all the spirit of a boy and she had said that she wanted Little Ox's brother as an adopted elder brother. Then, thinking of Foxy Mum, felt that she would lose face and so abandoned the idea.

"Why?" asked Aroma.

Duidui said angrily, "It's all her fault. It seems she was a taxi dancer at the well-known Evening Fragrance Dance Hall. Her mum and dad didn't like her and wanted to give her to a rich man as a mistress. She ran away, she didn't want to be a concubine. That's what I secretly overheard Granddad telling Granny."

At that moment a small green snake flew out of the undergrowth, as if it had been flung like a little piece of colored rope. It landed on Duidui's shoulder then slid down her back onto the ground and slithered back into the undergrowth.

Duidui was paralyzed with fright. Utterly terrified she screamed and screamed during the night.

Her mother wanted to take her to the hospital but her grandfather, Brother Ah De, absolutely would not allow it and said, "Duidui is a tender shoot of the Wu family and Wu blood runs in her veins. If I say she can't go, she can't go."

It later emerged that he was afraid that his precious granddaughter would be infected with other people's diseases if she went to hospital.

Back at school on Monday, teacher Chen looked at the desk occupied by Aroma and Little Ox and discovered a strange phenomenon: Aroma and Little Ox were sitting back to back and, rather as if they had carelessly run into each other, they pushed at each other with their elbows to show their determination to keep apart.

Teacher Chen told them to make it up with each other. She didn't know it but this was impossible. Aroma had found out from Runthead that Little Ox was raising the little green snake that had been flung out of the undergrowth. He had been lying in there teaching it to catch frogs when he heard Duidui discussing how Foxy Mum had been a taxi dancer and, in a rage, had flung the snake at her.

Aroma was incensed by Little Ox's roughness and the fright he had given Duidui and herself. He had been nasty to Duidui and now she was ill at home.

Teacher Chen said, "Little Ox, you must live in friendship with Aroma."

"Yes," said Little Ox, very respectfully, bending forward from the waist.

Teacher Chen was still not content and asked Little Ox, "Do you fully understand the reason for solidarity with classmates?"

"Fully understand," replied Little Ox firmly.

Teacher Chen sighed and said to Aroma, "Now it's your turn. Do you understand the reason here?"

Aroma, puffing with anger, said, "He obviously won't do it. The fact that he threw a green snake at Duidui and me just can't be tossed aside."

"Time. Time will resolve everything," said Teacher Chen. "You, Little Ox, apologize to Duidui and do not misbehave in future."

"Right," said Little Ox obediently.

Teacher Chen pulled Aroma towards her and then told them both the story of the three brothers breaking chopsticks. She said, "Three brothers each took up a chopstick and snapped it in half just like that. Next they took a bundle of chopsticks but it wasn't the same and none of them could break the chopsticks. Then the three brothers realized that it was even more the same with people: as with chopsticks, solidarity increased strength."

Little Ox couldn't refrain from interrupting, "There are three brothers in the story, there are five in my family, we all stick together."

Little Ox's face always bore an expression of pride when he mentioned that his family had five brothers. In fact, he was only good to his three elder brothers and was loyally devoted to them, but he looked down on Runthead, his younger brother.

Teacher Chen was very satisfied and left with relief.

Little Ox flew into a rage, saying that Runthead was soft in the head, had no guts, and had been led astray by Aroma. He had even told Aroma the story of him throwing the green snake at Duidui.

Little Ox thumped the table, paid no attention at all to Aroma and said that she was a goblin and a tigress.

Aroma went home at lunchtime to eat and by the entrance to the post office at Sinan Road she saw the old man who wrote letters for clients. How well written his brush characters were. Just as she was looking at them enthusiastically somebody trod on her foot. She discovered that it was Little Ox so she gave him a kick.

Seeing Aroma coming to kick him, he shouted at her, "Get lost, this is our territory, we come here every day."

Changxin happened to be alongside Little Ox and laughed when he saw this scene. In order to avoid embarrassment Little Ox said, "No, don't you get lost, I'll get lost," and flew off.

"There's nothing he can do when he comes across you," said Changxin. "He says you have a killer's club and he's frightened you will tell everybody about the green snake. Brother Ah De would be sure to go to his home and pick a fight."

Changxin who normally had little to say had said a great deal at one go and Aroma thought then how good it would be if she really had a killer's club. She could be someone amazing and could subjugate Little Ox.

It was hoped that this episode would make Little Ox more obedient in the future.

Washing in Soup

Hehuan came over in class and greeted Aroma. She was a quiet, sweet-voiced girl with white skin and a fringe. She was as sweet as pumpkin porridge. The pens and pencils she used were the best that could be found. Her clothes and her diary too had a fragrance: when she approached it surrounded her, wafting to and fro but never leaving her.

Hehuan was straightforward and quick in speech. It was said that she had read *Pravda*. None of the other children in the class had read *Pravda* and none of them knew what *Pravda* was. Consequently they were even more in awe of her.

Hehuan was Changxin's cousin. Her father was ill with a liver complaint that he was afraid he might give to her, and so he had sent her to live with Changxin's family. Despite living with her mother's brother's family she was both adorable and adored and treated like a princess by her uncle and aunt. She was a little arrogant and thought that boys of her age were stupid, dirty and brainless. The only one who was any good was her cousin Changxin.

She warned Aroma not to use the "sun water" in Auntie Mai's wooden bucket saying, "For heaven's sake don't use it, remember."

"Why not?" Aroma asked.

Hehuan giggled and said, "It's not water, it's soup."

Auntie Mai liked water that had been heated in the sun, saying that at home there had been a spring of pure, sweet water. But Little Ox and the others laughed at her and said that her bucket was like the breaking of waves on a lake.

"Little Ox sneakily lifted the lid on the bucket and put in the little green snake to swim around, as well as adding taste powder, saccharine and peppers, just like making a real soup. I can't bear to see him be so nasty," said Hehuan.

Aroma went in search of Little Ox who was with a crowd of other boys. When he saw her coming he pretended that nothing had happened.

"Why are you so annoying?" asked Aroma.

"Serves her right," Little Ox's arrogant gaze pierced Aroma uncomfortably. Still mocking Auntie Mai he said, "I put in a handful of salt this morning. She likes washing in soup and in a while her body will be salty all over."

Auntie Mai could not put up with Little Ox's rude behavior and often had to come to the aid of Aroma and Didi. There had been a number of times when she had told tales of Little Ox in front of Foxy Dad and as a consequence Little Ox hated her.

"You're taking revenge," Aroma said. "You think that Auntie Mai interferes in things that are none of her business."

Little Ox was much pleased with himself. He had not got the sunflower and so had switched his anger to Auntie Mai and said, "This is called rewarding evil with evil."

Aroma was reduced to tears of anger but she was not going to allow Auntie Mai to be done down. Auntie Mai learnt about this very soon. It was unbearable and she went to Foxy Dad to have it out.

Foxy Dad was furious at what he heard and said angrily, "I'll teach him a lesson. It's all on account of being spoiled rotten by his mother."

Foxy Mum quickly made amends to Auntie Mai saying, "Little wretch, he's a little devil."

In a while an exasperated Foxy Dad got hold of Little Ox and was raising his hand to teach him a lesson when Foxy Mum rushed over and said, "I'll help Auntie Mai vent her anger. I'll do it, such a lawless little devil."

With a mouthful of fierce phrases she loudly cursed the daylight from the sky but held back Foxy Dad's arm whilst interposing her own body to protect Little Ox.

"All thunder and no rain ... I don't understand her. She favors Little Ox over everybody," Auntie Mai whispered as, rather embarrassed, she went to intercede for Little Ox.

"There's no need for that," said Auntie Mai.

"No," said Foxy Mum, "I must still help you to vent your anger. This little devil, how dare he do this to you? I'm not forgiving him."

"Enough. I didn't want you to beat your child," said Auntie Mai. "It's terrible. Little Ox gives me such supercilious looks. I don't know what he blames me for."

But later Little Ox was indeed taught a lesson, by his elder brother who had been born in the year of the tiger. This elder brother was handsome and was studying at a famous university and his demands on his younger brothers were high. If he discovered that they had been making trouble and had brought shame on the family, there was no messing about. His hand was hard and he gave Little Ox a roasting.

Little Ox did not hate his elder brother so in his rage and humiliation turned his hatred on Auntie Mai and Runthead.

That morning Didi and Runthead went very early to the garden to play and as an adventure they climbed into the magnolia tree and flung a rope on to Duidui's balcony. They wanted Duidui to tie the end to the railings. They had already tied their end to a tree branch. The result was that by accident Little Ox saw it and cut the rope.

Seeing the disappointment on the faces of the two young ones Little Ox was very pleased with himself.

Aroma saw this with her eyes and felt anger with her heart.

During the midday break at school Aroma went to the kindergarten to see Didi. Didi and Runthead had just had their lunch and, although their teacher had told them to take a nap, they were still running about and playing on the slide. One was at the top and one was climbing up from the opposite direction to prevent the other from sliding down. They were playing away happily, laughing and giggling.

"Bastard!" the sound of a single curse. It was Little Ox who had brought along Suiping. Little Ox ordered Runthead to go back to the teacher straight away but Runthead was unwilling and just stood there. Little Ox put on a display of power and kicked him in the crotch. There was an expression of great pain on Runthead's face. He covered himself with his hands but dared not say anything.

Aroma said, "You're evil-minded, Little Ox."

"You dare curse me, you tigress."

Somehow or other the two fell to trading blows. At this point Didi and Runthead also piled in and helped Aroma secure Little Ox's legs.

"Good. Let them all come. You've got my legs," said Little Ox, "but I'll throw a knapsack at you."

Suiping saw what was happening and rushed off to find Teacher Chen. Suiping was good-natured, talked a lot and was excitable. He was always busy and in a hurry and he got on well with Changxin and worshipped the ground he walked on.

Teacher Chen hurried over. She had a pretty face and was attractive, rather like the dance teacher, but she was very serious and would sigh repeatedly when telling off children for fidgeting. If anybody contradicted her in class, or failed to hand in their homework, or interrupted her lesson, she would get worked up and treat it as an earth-shattering event. If anybody repeated the offence then they were being cheeky and she would immediately go and see their parents.

Teacher Chen called Aroma and Little Ox into the office and said that when she was small she had once been late and the teacher had marked her name, and she still remembered it. When she recalled how she had been criticized when she was small a blush appeared on her cheeks.

"Fighting in public is very bad. How could you pretend that nothing was the matter?"

She made them write a self-examination right there in the office. If they didn't finish it they would not be allowed to rejoin the class.

Little Ox appeared to be quite skilled in writing a self-examination and threw one together just like that. Aroma wrote a few sentences and stopped because she wanted to know what Little Ox was writing, but since they had just had a fight she was too embarrassed to go and look.

Later, Teacher Chen came in to the office and saw Aroma standing by the desk tearing something up into very small pieces so as to leave nothing behind.

"Aroma, what are you doing?"

"I don't like writing this self-examination. I can't write it."

"Use your brain. If you don't it will get rusty and become worthless."

"I'm not not using my brain. It's that I just don't want to write that sort of thing," said Aroma.

Aroma was a perceptive and sensitive child and henceforward took a dislike to Teacher Chen, the literature and language teacher. Consequently, her literature and language grades were very bad. She liked Teacher Dong who taught arithmetic and so her arithmetic grades were a little better.

"It still has to be written. The next lesson is composition but you must stay here, Aroma, and carry on writing," said Teacher Chen.

A Gift Called "Recompense"

After the composition lesson Suiping and Changxin came to see Aroma, dragging Little Ox along with them and saying to him in front of her, "You go and find Teacher Chen and tell her the truth: that Aroma was coming to rescue somebody else who was being bullied."

Little Ox said, "I'm not going to, not unless you give me a box of presents."

"Go on, go on," said Changxin.

In the end, Little Ox went and Teacher Chen forgave Aroma and let her off writing the self-examination.

However, Aroma no longer wanted to share a desk with Little Ox. She wanted to share with Changxin instead. He was neat, didn't talk too much and was likeable and intelligent. Dad didn't approve of Aroma changing desks straightaway. He wanted Aroma to learn how to get on with Little Ox. Changxin found out and acting the conciliator asked Little Ox, "Do you want to change desks?"

Little Ox replied, "No need to change."

Aroma said, "That's good. Then you won't need to sneer at

people, you won't need to say 'tigress.'"

Little Ox was reluctant and said, "You still owe me a box of presents. Give them to me and I'll promise."

"What kind of presents do you want in your box?"

"I want really heavy presents," said Little Ox.

"Good, you'll get them. There will certainly be very heavy things in the box," said Aroma happily.

"Not too heavy, no coal or stones," said Little Ox, stuck between doubt and belief. "I want very light presents."

"Light is as light does," said Aroma. "I'll give you a box of gifts of recompense."

"What's a gift of recompense? Where do you get recompense from?"

"I'll find a way," said Aroma.

"Impossible, you're lying," said Little Ox. "What's recompense?"

Aroma did not answer.

The boys were much interested and said, "It's probably a codename."

The next day, Aroma came to school carrying a very square, sealed paper box. She put it on Little Ox's desk and he rushed up and asked, "What is it?"

"It's a gift of recompense," said Aroma.

Little Ox picked up the paper box and shook it, saying, "It's very light, there's nothing in it, it's just air isn't it?"

Aroma just said, "It's up to you," and walked off.

Little Ox was not satisfied and, asking Suiping for a knife, cut the sealing tape and soon had the box unwrapped.

He opened the box, peered in and, unable to restrain himself, shouted, "It's ants!"

The assembled ants came climbing out of the paper box on their way back to their nest. In no time at all they had crawled majestically all over his desk, his books and his pens and pencils and even onto him too—columns of ants were crawling over his shoulders and arms.

"It's really frightening," Little Ox shouted as he brushed at his clothes. "It's an army of ants and two of them are boring into my belly button."

"This is a gift of recompense," Aroma said, "a revenge present. Who asked you to throw a snake at Duidui and to bully Runthead?"

Teacher Chen saw it and said, "My very scalp tingles. Heavens, I can't teach you. I've never met a girl as wild as you."

Aroma said not a word and returned disconsolately home. When she arrived she thought she would find Duidui and tell her about giving the "revenge gift" to Little Ox. But Duidui's granny told her that Duidui was better and had gone back to school.

Aroma felt very much alone during the day. Would life go on like this? When she was sad she thought about strange things, for example, what would it be like if one day rabbits lost their fur? She smiled at this and was happy for a little while.

Aroma was still holed up at home in the afternoon and when particularly miserable practiced walking on her hands.

Aunti Mai saw her and said, "Stop it, stop it, you're all topsy-turvy."

Aroma's father very soon learned what had happened because Teacher Chen told him. He was angry and said to Aroma, "You mustn't be so headstrong. You're grown-up already."

"Please don't be angry," said Aroma. "I'm a bit angry with myself now. I just wanted to be cleverer and fiercer than Little Ox."

On Sunday Dad took Aroma to see Teacher Chen for a talk. He told Aroma to wait at the door of a cooked food shop called "Wu Ahsi" while he went to buy some fruit.

Teacher Chen lived on a market street. It was very narrow but it was crowded with shop fronts and squeezed in on either side were restaurants, bathhouses and shops that sold hot water. There was a narrow grocery store. The shop itself was full but a rectangular table had been set up facing the street and laid out on this stall were chicken-feather dusters and scrubbing brushes. Underneath the table there were grindstones and wooden buckets on legs. The unceasing river of people that flowed past had to lean away as their trouser legs brushed against the local goods.

Aroma wandered around the vicinity and looked at the peepshow and then came back and stood on tiptoe and looked up to see if the signboard of the shop had "Wu Ahsi Cooked Foods" written on it but, as a result, she was pushed a long way forward by the press of impatient pedestrians behind her. She was worried and tried to push back but was unexpectedly given a shove by someone, lost her balance and fell into a large grass nest in the grocery store. The owner of the store smoothly replaced the lid of the nest and said with a laugh, "Why don't you live in here?"

Aroma was tired of standing and settled down quietly for a rest saying, "Good, I'll be the princess of the nest."

The owner laughed, "What an innocent child you are. That's used for covering pots of cooked rice."

Aroma went back to "Wu Ahsi Cooked Foods" but couldn't see her dad and thought that perhaps he had gone to see Teacher Chen by himself. Then she went searching herself.

Mr. Egg Roll

On the way, Aroma saw somebody who smiled at her and said, "So you're here?"

Aroma thought she knew him and had come across him somewhere before. He was good-looking but dressed any old how. His face was as thin as a twisted salty doughnut but he was doing something really interesting: he was making egg rolls.

He had a large bucket of flour paste and an iron hotplate beside which was a basket of eggshells. He had a semi-transparent glove on his left hand but his right hand was bare. He subconsciously raised his left hand and mixed the flour paste with a long wooden ladle grasped in his right hand, saying to Aroma the while, "This is a flour paste made of eggs and white sugar."

"You know me, don't you?" Aroma asked. "Otherwise you shouldn't be speaking to me."

He laughed and, waiting until he had finished mixing the paste, said, "Of course I do. You once told me that your sunflower could dance."

"I remember. You came to Springwater Lane, but you left," said Aroma. "You shouldn't have left in such a hurry."

He spread a little oil on the hotplate and then poured on half a ladle of paste which, when it had been evenly spread, he swiftly turned and cooked and then rolled up with his left hand while it was still soft.

"Your right hand is too busy," said Aroma.

"True," he said, "that's what I thought as well."

"Why does your left hand do just one thing?" Aroma continued. "It could work just as hard as your right."

"It's a habit. One can't stop when it's busy and the other is used to being idle," he said. "It's like the people and things in the world we live in. It's all fixed."

"I'd like to help your right hand," Aroma said. "Can I?"

"Of course, but you must be careful not to cough and not to sneeze," he said. "It should be as clean as if you were wearing a surgical mask."

Aroma helped mix the paste, which was very stiff and needed a lot of strength to mix properly. Ladling out the right amount of paste was difficult too. She once ladled out too much and it made a huge egg roll.

Aroma quickly compromised and said, "I wanted to make a mother roll."

"That's it, you've done it," he said. "What you say is very interesting. I'm going to call you 'Little Egg Roll,' all right?"

"Then I'll call you 'Mr. Egg Roll.'"

"Agreed. It's a good name and easy to remember," said Mr. Egg Roll, "however, we ought to make our egg rolls a little better-looking."

Afraid that Mr. Egg Roll didn't want her to continue, Aroma ladled out too little, resulting in a small egg roll, quite tiny in fact.

Mr. Egg Roll said, "What would you say that is?"

Aroma said, "It's a baby egg roll produced by mother egg roll."

Mr. Egg Roll was a kind man and scored a level mark on the ladle: paste up to that line would produce really good egg rolls.

"This is the knack of doing things," said Mr. Egg Roll. "If you have the knack, nothing is difficult."

"Truly, you just need the knack."

"No," he said, "having the knack is a start, but to do things to their best is not easy and requires work, brains and method."

When Dad and Teacher Chen at last found her after a frantic search, they saw Aroma with an apron tied round her waist and her chin smudged with flour paste but very happy because she had made lots of egg rolls. The more she made the faster she got and they were now piled high.

She had even imitated the call of "Wang Ahda" who sold fried Gingko nuts: "Egg rolls, egg rolls, come and buy, piping hot to scorch your hand and delicious to taste! Buy some for your son or for your daughter if you haven't got a son!" She deliberately changed "piping hot" to "bibing tot" and "delicious to taste" to "malicious to waste" but she didn't like to make a gasping sound and she didn't like making the passersby soft-hearted.

"I'll have two catties of egg rolls," sad a fat uncle passing by. "Little girl, you sing very well, just like a little bird."

Aroma looked at the fat uncle who wanted to buy two big bags at one go and said, "Why do you want to buy so many? They'll be too heavy to carry."

"It's you who made me buy them when I heard your song."

"But ... it's taken a lot of trouble to make just a few piles. Wouldn't it be a good thing if even more people had a chance of tasting them?" asked Aroma.

"Is she your daughter?" the uncle asked Mr. Egg Roll. "She's a lot of fun. Right, I'll have one catty."

After the fat uncle had gone Aroma had an idea: she piled up the rolls she had made like building blocks, some in the shape of a pagoda, some like little houses and some like log rafts so that customers could choose a pagoda or a house or a raft.

But Dad and Teacher Chen had arrived.

Aroma performed an introduction, "This is my good friend Mr. Egg Roll."

The two adults measured up Mr. Egg Roll with some curiosity. They knew nothing of him or why he had that kind of name or how he had become so closely acquainted with Aroma.

Mr. Egg Roll didn't actively greet them but hurriedly wrapped up the "mother roll" and "baby roll" and told Aroma to take them home to eat, saying, "Take the fruits of your labor."

Aroma opened the paper bag and took it to show Teacher Chen, but Teacher Chen just looked and said nothing.

Aroma still wanted to say something and so told Teacher Chen, "If you want to make egg rolls the same size, the amount of flour paste you ladle out mustn't be too much or too little."

Finally Teacher Chen became irritated and said, "Are you going to go on just talking about flour paste?"

Aroma was rendered speechless, as if she had been struck with a club. It was best to keep silent.

The three of them went to Teacher Chen's home, in a building that spanned the street from one side of the alley to the other. It was rather like a sort of bridged corridor but sealed off at both ends. People entering or leaving the alley had to pass under the building.

Teacher Chen had no mother or father but lived alone with her younger brother whose legs had been affected by polio. He was in a wheelchair, wearing a blue uniform, a neat, well-behaved boy. He was arranging a collection of matchboxes and pictures, treasures that filled two large drawers.

"Good morning, sir," he said, noticing that there were only a few matches left in Aroma's father's matchbox and eyeing it.

Aroma's father asked, "Would you like this matchbox for your collection?"

"Yes, I'd be very happy to have it," said the boy. "Have you just smoked an Albanian cigarette?"

"How do you know?" Aroma's father asked. "My neighbor gave me one this morning. I just took a couple of puffs and put it out."

"I can detect the smell," said the boy. "The smell of tobacco lingers in the lining of people's clothes."

However, Teacher Chen did not like her younger brother collecting matchboxes and complained that sooner or later he would burn the house down.

The table was all homework exercise books and a bottle of ink as well. As she was speaking, Teacher Chen found Hehuan's exercise book and showed it to Aroma's father, "Aroma's very clever as well, no less clever than Hehuan, if only she could learn from her."

Aroma was uncomfortable. She did not like being criticized in front of the boy by Teacher Chen and her stomach immediately played up. She said, "My stomach aches."

"Does it?" Dad asked.

Her stomach was aching and Aroma, desperate to get away, said, "It aches a lot."

Dad carried Aroma home on his back. When they arrived home Dad himself had chest pains and went to the hospital. He returned after a long time with a laboratory test slip.

Mum said, "It doesn't look too good, I'll go with you for an examination at the main hospital."

Aroma felt a confused sense of upset and fear and believed that she had brought this on her father. It was her fault. It had happened because of her father's anger.

Feeling a stinging sensation in her eyes she rushed off to the little garden and wept alone.

Suddenly, something fell softly on her shoulder. It was Duidui's dog, called Fulai, a soft toy obviously.

Aroma looked up and couldn't see anything but in a little while there was the sound of giggling that was clearly Duidui. She was standing on the little narrow balcony with the little red hat on her head, her body flat as if inlaid in a landscape on a wall.

Duidui ran down to retrieve Fulai the dog, saw Aroma in silent tears and asked her what the matter was. Aroma told her what was on her mind. Duidui felt she didn't quite understand and said, "But nothing's happened."

"That's not correct," said Aroma. "I'm very upset and sad."

Duidui's way of comforting Aroma was rather special. She puckered up her mouth and kissed her. Aroma felt very awkward but Duidui thought nothing of it. When she was sad she liked people to kiss her and thought Aroma was the same.

Later Duidui brought some rushes that she broke into lengths so that Aroma could suck nectar through a straw. Aroma shook her head.

"Never mind," said Duidui indignantly, "I was just trying to cheer you up."

Duidui left Aroma alone and when she saw Snow White the cat, she brought her over saying that she was chubby, and gave her the nectar to taste. She fed Fulai the toy dog as well and giggled, "He looks very greedy but he mustn't dribble."

Aroma laughed and said, "You aren't angry?"

Duidui shook her head and pouting as if wronged said, "What are you talking about?"

Neither of the two girls really knew what the other was thinking but they were good friends because between them there was enough love, understanding and confidence. Very soon they were reconciled.

Snow White Acquires Skills

Just as Aroma's stomachache was getting better she developed a fever. It was tonsillitis and her tonsils oozed pus. When she spoke her throat hurt as if it were being bitten by an insect. When she ate, it was as if her throat was being scraped by a blunt knife.

Aroma's mother went to Duidui's mother for help. Duidui's mum introduced her to a well-known doctor, alas not Dr. Bag. Had it been him, Aroma would have been easier in her mind. She would have liked to see Dr. Bag, a doctor she knew and whose adopted son, Bag Bum, she knew as well.

The hospital corridor smelt of ethanol. Auntie Mai who was with her liked the smell. She closed her plump mouth tight and breathed in and out through her nostrils.

The doctor said that he wanted to remove the tonsils. Otherwise the condition would worsen. He said, "The tonsils are of almost no use to the body, there is no obstacle to removal. Once removed there will be no re-occurrence of tonsillitis, it will be finished for good."

Mum asked, "Will the wound ache unbearably?"

"There will be a burning sensation after surgery. Generally, for children, swallowing ice cream in addition to medication can reduce the pain. It will pass after a few days."

"Are you saying that I should swallow White Snow brand ice cream?" Aroma asked with delight.

"You can," said the doctor.

"That's good," Aroma said. "Doctor, please go gently in the operation."

"What! If the vocal chords are cut she'll be dumb, won't she?" interjected Auntie Mai. "This operation is like cutting the gills out of a fish. I couldn't bear to part with them. Would heaven give us something we didn't need? The things heaven give us are there and who's to say that one day they might not come in handy? If Aroma's tonsils flare up again, I'll look after her. I always look after her well. I don't let her kick off her quilt at night. I won't let them flare up again."

There was nothing the doctor could say to this firecracker speech.

So Auntie Mai carried Aroma home on her back. Later, using some folk remedy from goodness knows where, she made a solution of salt and boric acid for Aroma to use to wash out her throat and treat the inflammation.

Changxin thought that Aroma had had the operation and brought over the family's German-made fan, saying that they were lending it to Aroma for her throat. Auntie Mai wouldn't let Aroma talk and kept her in bed to rest for the sake of her tonsils. If needs be she used sign language and so Aroma was only able to gesture her thanks to Changxin. Fortunately Changxin understood her gestures.

On the third day, Aroma felt only slight pain in the throat.

Dad was delighted and as a reward took Aroma to the cinema. Didi went as well. The Russian film was about the story of the girl who tamed a tiger. The girl was called Lena. She could make the tiger narrow its eyes and behave as well as a little cat. At a gesture or a glance the tiger would brave fire and water for her.

Didi said, "It would have been good if she'd been a man. She would have been more famous than Wu Song who killed a tiger with his bare hands."

"It's best she's a girl. With brass buttons on her jacket, beautiful and dangerous," Aroma said.

Dreamy Aroma was showing that she wanted to be the greatest animal trainer in the world.

Aroma thought that there was nothing wrong with this. There were a lot of children who were at school now because they liked it. They thought studying was the most interesting thing in the world. But Aroma was not holed up in a classroom with a teacher and a lot of others. She was doing something else. She wanted to be like Lena, with Lena's big eyes, in jodhpurs, and able to make a tiger crouch at her feet like a cat.

There was no tiger for Aroma to train but she was still intent on being the girl who tamed a tiger.

Didi felt she could start by training a cat and Aroma agreed it was the best she could do. She picked up Snow White and whirled round and round to toughen up her courage and her savage instincts. She thought the name that Didi had given her was no good. It was just peculiar and not the least dangerous sounding. If the cat had been called White Thunderbolt or White Fur it would have been very different.

"You're a tiger, you're a tiger," she said to her. Because she had linked her dreams to the cat, she thought she would understand and realize that she was a tiger.

But Snow White was motivated by self-interest. She was attached to Auntie Mai, probably because she liked eating the fish with rice that she cooked. So she struggled in Aroma's embrace, yowling in protest. Aroma paid no attention and turned faster and faster like a windmill in a storm.

There were stars in front of her eyes and Aroma turned her head to try and stop but couldn't. As a result both she and the cat fell over. Snow White then mistook Aroma for an enemy who was trying to harm her, summoned up her strength, unsheathed her claws and made her fur stand on end so that she appeared twice her normal size.

"She's turned into a tiger!" Aroma called in delight.

"You've really done it!" shouted Didi. Nothing today had been so much fun.

Snow White was scared. Her whiskers kept twitching and the two incisors in her mouth stuck out in a show of extreme alarm.

Thereafter she hid when she saw the two of them. Sometimes she hid under the bed and wouldn't come out, probably thinking that there was something suspicious about them.

Aroma was very put out. Auntie Mai teased her and said, "I'll be a tiger for you." She then roared like a tiger.

Aroma pushed at Auntie Mai. She really didn't want Auntie Mai to be a tiger. If she learned to bite people, and the movements of how to do a salutation, she would know everything and that would be no fun at all.

Auntie Mai laughed, and said that Snow White would only be particularly obedient when she was hungry. She then helped devise a feeding strategy and supplied some specially made dried fish as a nutritious meal, the dried fish that Snow White loved.

In a while Snow White felt hungry and came looking for Auntie Mai, circling round her and rubbing her thick fur against her legs.

Auntie Mai gave Aroma the dried fish to feed to her. At the beginning she was standoffish but when Aroma stroked and petted her she gave in.

Aroma set up a pole as a bar and signaled Snow White to stand on her hind legs. She seemed to enjoy it and stood for a long time. She was really talented and learned how to obey a spoken command in a day. When Aroma called out "salute" she stood up at once and put her forepaws together in a greeting.

"There's as much fun in training a cat as in training a tiger," said Aroma.

But once having learned how to salute, Snow White didn't want to do it again. If a green-headed fly flew past she would chase it. When Aroma ordered her back she suddenly got fed up and took no notice.

It was only at feeding time that she slowly paid attention. She very quickly learned to push the catch on the window so that she could open it.

Didi rushed over to stop it. He said that Snow White was a super-cat. It would be a pity to teach her things that humans could do already. She should be taught things that they couldn't do, for example turning somersaults in the air, walking a tightrope, walking on a ball and jumping through a fire hoop.

"An instant success," said Didi in the accents of a comedy duologue, "with the blessing of the world's number one living Buddha."

But Snow White was a real freak. When Aroma taught her high jumping and showed her how, she wouldn't learn properly but stood there, watching curiously as Aroma jumped about. Aroma was in a sweat of anxiety. She pushed her to jump but she just lay down as if stuck to the floor by suckers. Perhaps she believed that she had already mastered all Aroma's skills and there was now no further need for obedience.

Aroma felt that Didi had a point after all: she should not simply teach her human skills, but skills that were more difficult. She wanted her to abandon everything she had learned the previous day and to start again from the beginning. She started to teach her in reverse, saying "salute" and then tapping her on the head or pulling her short tail like a little demon.

But little Snow White got angry as well and growled, "Wu, wu, wu, wu ..."

Auntie Mai said to Aroma, "Will you give up? You're so fierce, are you trying to kill her? She thinks you're a wolf."

"There's nothing I can do," said Aroma, "unless you could make me a mask so that she doesn't know who's training her."

Auntie Mai set to and made Aroma a fierce wolf mask out of cardboard, and put it on for her.

Every time Aroma trained Snow White she hid away while putting on the wolf mask. She was afraid that otherwise Snow White might remember her with hatred.

This little cat, Snow White, understood human nature and was exceedingly intelligent but her brain was like a muscle. It couldn't change just like that. If you said a word to her that sounded like "salute," for example "commute" or "pollute" or "fruit" or "brute," she would perform the movement for "salute." Except that when she did it in front of Aroma when she was wearing the wolf mask, she dared not perform the "salute" movement but liked to perform the "sucker" movement instead.

Didi was anxious to put on a cat training show and he and Runthead had put up posters all over Springwater Lane.

Aroma turned the chest of drawers upside down. If she saw clothes with brass buttons she cut the buttons off and eventually found twenty-five. She stitched them all over her jacket, making it very wrinkled. Hanging by threads, the brass buttons clashed together as she walked and produced a *ding-dong* sound.

Anyway, Aroma had now acquired a tiger-training outfit like Lena's.

Nevertheless, shouldn't dearly beloved younger brother Didi have a suit as well? She also thought of one for Runthead but, alas, all the buttons had been used up and there were no more to be found. All she could do was cut the brass buttons off her father's old army uniform.

"I also want to teach Snow White cat-speak comedy," said Didi. "There's nothing wrong in a cat doing a comedy duologue."

Once the two training outfits had been made, Aroma planned on going to school. Her throat was no longer painful and she could shout without difficulty.

But that morning, just as she came out of the door with her satchel on her back, somebody stopped her and asked about the cat, saying that they had seen the posters and had come specially.

It was Snow White's real owner, a good-looking lady.

Didi was distressed to the point of tears and said, "No. no, we're cat training."

"He will cry himself to death," said Auntie Mai, her heart aching with love, "could he keep her for a little longer?"

Aroma helpfully interceded, "We've spent a lot of time teaching her how to open the window."

The lady said, "Open the window? She can open the door as well, and say bye-bye, and stand on her hind paws, and stand on her head, and play dead, and do a salutation, and do a fox dance. Little Mary's very able, she learns things in an instant."

No wonder!!! So she'd been able to do these tricks all along.

Didi was all the more unwilling to give her up and said, "She's so clever she's bound to be able to do comedy duologues."

He clung to Snow White tightly and shouted at anybody who tried to persuade him. Everybody felt that things had reached an impasse and Aroma's father was telephoned to come home and sort it out.

At that moment the pretty lady's daughter rushed up.

This angelic little girl was called Jenny and had been brought by the pretty lady. She embraced Didi's legs with soft white arms and said politely, "Elder Brother, please give my little cat back to me."

Didi had been moved by the little girl and returned Snow White to her.

After Jenny and her mother had left Didi collapsed and slept the whole day without taking food. Aroma woke him when it was dark and discovered that his hair was standing on end, that the corners of his eyes were drooping and that to everybody's surprise his little face was a deep yellow.

"How are you?"

"I don't feel well here," Didi pointed to his chest, "just now I dreamt about Snow White."

Aroma loved him dearly. To make him forget his pain she donned the cat trainer's outfit and imitated Snow White's comical movements as she asked, "Did she do ballet like this?"

"Not like that, her paws went like this," Didi gestured as he spoke. He was a brilliant mimic and a natural performer.

"Right, I'll imitate what she does when she washes her face," said Aroma enthusiastically.

Just at that moment Teacher Chen arrived on a home visit and beheld the child who had not appeared in school for several days, cavorting around, strangely clad in clothes bedecked with brass buttons.

A Decision to Leave School

"Why have you not been to school?" Teacher Chen asked.

"I was wanting to come but something happened. My brother was ill and there was something else ... a lady came early this morning ..."

"Your brother was ill? Are you a doctor?" Teacher Chen demanded.

"I'm not. But he's in a pitiful ... he ..."

"Don't go on. You're a truant."

Teacher Chen did not intend to listen to any more of Aroma's explanations and sat waiting for Aroma's mother and father to come home. Later she talked to them about early year education and how to turn bad children into good ones. She said, "You have to be strict with Aroma, very strict and even stricter."

After she left, Auntie Mai patted her chest and said, "That Teacher Chen, she's awful, she tears people off a real strip. The moment she went all po-faced it nearly gave me a heart attack. Aiya, she gave Sir and Madam a real telling off."

"Don't talk like that. Teacher Chen was anxious and upset," said Dad.

Mum sighed.

Aroma rushed out and, in the little garden country, leant down in the night air and said to the sunflower, "I don't blame you for not dancing." She wept as she spoke and her tears dropped like dewdrops of crystal onto the slightly closed, furled petals in the flowerpot.

The sunflower seemed very independent. Was it looking at the tall trees and the even higher sky? Perhaps it felt insignificant and had a fantasy that it could grow as tall as a tree and that when it could look at the sky from mid-air the view would not be the same.

What Teacher Chen had said had been deeply wounding. Aroma did not understand why she would not let her say everything that was on her mind. She would have been able to talk for a long time. There was so much on her mind. It was nearly full and about to overflow.

Just then, she heard Didi shout from inside, "I feel as if there's a huge stone pressing on my chest."

Moments later Auntie Mai, wiping away her tears, rushed into the little garden, saw Aroma and said, "How heartless those people were to carry Snow White off. See, Didi is not eating or drinking. How can this be right?"

Aroma was upset for her own sake and for Didi: how much worse was it to have a huge stone weighing on your heart?

That night, amidst the tidal snoring of Auntie Mai, Aroma felt that she was floating dizzily on the sea.

In the morning Aroma was running a high temperature again. It was the tonsils still causing trouble. Aroma's dad decided she should have the operation but Mum and Auntie Mai were hesitant and unwilling. They felt that to remove anything from Aroma's little body would be a tragedy. Moreover, Mum was afraid of complications.

They all went to the hospital where the doctor had prepared a room. Dad wanted to carry on with the procedure but their minds were in a complete whirl and they stopped Dad, deciding for the moment not to go ahead with the operation but to take Aroma home.

They took it in turns to carry Aroma on their backs. They didn't allow her to walk but let her hang swaying with her feet dangling. They gently rubbed her head and were extremely affectionate and treated her like a shining jewel that had just been recovered.

During the days that Aroma was ill at home she received the

love and attention due to a princess. Mum never left her side and stingy Auntie Mai was transformed. Aroma had but to say that she felt like eating something and Auntie Mai would fly out and buy it without dawdling on the way back. She bought the square egg rolls that Aroma liked and a kind of steamed Baiyuan egg cake as well. In addition there were Purple Brand chocolate ice cream bars and Fujian meat rolls.

"You're so generous," Aroma said.

"True," said Auntie Mai, "when the family baby is ill, I'll give anything."

Aroma said, "It would be wonderful if you could always be as generous as this."

"Not possible. When you're better there'll be no asking for things all over the place," Auntie Mai said firmly. "I'm no enemy of money but it's a crime to squander it ..."

While Aroma was running a temperature nobody had taken much notice of Didi. This had been to the good. He had slowly got over the loss of Snow White and begun to get better, except that at night he wouldn't let Auntie Mai close the door, saying that Snow White was bound to escape and come back.

Didi performed comedy duologues for Aroma every day until *Waiters from Everywhere* was on its seventh performance! He did it with enthusiasm each time and in a multitude of dialects and accents so as to make Aroma laugh happily and recover quickly.

"Haha, haha," gurgled Aroma.

In fact Aroma had heard this particular duologue so many times that her ears had grown calluses. But she still enjoyed it and laughed at it. Didi was adept at getting a laugh. He rushed home each time and grabbed something with which to act out the various waiters' accents.

He used a different prop each time and improvised with anything that was at hand. Once it was a bundle of chopsticks, another time it was a melon and on one occasion, unable to find anything, he shouldered a sack of rice flour though he later punctured the sack. The worst time of all was when he performed with a stack of bowls and smashed the lot.

Aroma was really happy. Everything that Didi did was for the sake of his sister. Aroma thought with pride that this was not something that other people could enjoy.

"A pair of idiots," was the way that Auntie Mai sometimes described the brother and sister. But it was said fondly, "No matter what, they are of one heart, that's good, like children I've brought up myself."

By the time she had recovered Aroma had become completely accustomed to family life. She would not be parted from any of it and no longer wanted to go to school. She said very firmly, "Please let me leave school."

Mum looked at the expression on Aroma's face and said quietly, "Perhaps it's for the best. Let her convalesce at home and then change schools, and when Didi goes to school next year, one can do year one and the other can do year two again."

"That's right. When you've changed schools, when the time comes, there'll be no need to see that Teacher Chen anymore." Auntie Mai went on reflectively, "when she's married and has children of her own she'll realize that being cruel to children has consequences."

With two stalwart supporters Aroma urged her father to withdraw her from school every day.

Be a Good Girl for Three Days

There was nothing that Dad could do and at last he wrote out the application for withdrawal. But before he sent it off to the school he said once more, "Why forget that you can win them over?"

Aroma shook her head.

Dad got up to his tricks and insisted on having a bet with her to see if she could go to school and be a good girl for three days. If, after three days, Aroma still wanted to leave then he would promise to say no more and send in the application at once.

Aroma had great regard for Dad because he had never

hurt her feelings but she didn't want to agree at once. She had a vague feeling that a rather different meaning lurked behind his understated language.

It so happened that that evening Hehuan and Changxin were rehearsing the play *The Greedy Little Bear* in the little garden country. They saw Aroma and urged her to accept the bet. They also asked her to hear their parts.

That evening at supper, Dad and Aroma sealed a pact to show that neither was going to cheat on it.

Aroma reckoned that it wasn't difficult to go back to school and behave well for three days. Once through that her life would change wonderfully, so she cheered up.

Aroma went back to school and because she thought that she would only be there for three days she was nice to everybody, rather like a guest. She was very moved to see her classmates so good to her and that they had forgotten the "revenge present" of the ant army. She had thought up some words of farewell but they remained hidden away in her heart for the very last moment of the three days.

She persevered through the first day. When she saw Little Ox, who shared her desk, playing with a knife she just said, "You need to be careful when you use that."

He said, "I'm practicing with a plastic knife, but I'll be using a real knife to harvest our sunflower." He went on to say that "our sunflower" was nearly fully-grown and so he guarded it when he had time. He also got the little green snake to loosen the earth for it.

The next day, believe it or not, Aroma was praised. During the class meeting Teacher Chen made everybody blow up balloons, saying that they would be decorating the stage for the following day's performance. The performance was very important and Head Teacher Zhang and the others would all be attending.

Aroma was happy to help because Head Teacher Zhang would be coming and she was Changxin's mum. She was very pretty and kind too. Aroma liked her. Moreover, Aroma would be leaving this collective in another day and thought that she would do a little more for it.

She blew up a very large balloon. Little Ox grabbed it to play with the moment it was full and then burst it.

She very much wanted to have a fight with him but then she thought about it: never mind, another day and she would no longer be sharing a desk with him. So she went off to blow up more balloons and blew her anger into the balloons and in a while all her pent up anger was exhausted. She blew up a lot of balloons that day, so many that her lips were swollen. When Teacher Chen saw it she was vey moved and went out of her way to praise Aroma.

Aroma was delighted to receive praise on a day when she was about to leave school, and from Teacher Chen too. She followed Teacher Chen around wanting to explain the business of Snow White to her once more but didn't know where to start and so left it.

At last the third day arrived, the day on which her bet with Dad was to be successfully concluded. There was to be the performance in the afternoon. Aroma felt this was a good idea. It could be her farewell to the school.

The item that her class had prepared was the play *The Greedy Little Bear*. Originally the performers were to have been Hehuan and Changxin but in the afternoon Hehuan had developed a violent stomachache and the school doctor, suspecting appendicitis, would not let her perform.

"Can anybody take over from Hehuan?" Teacher Chen asked anxiously.

"I can," said Aroma.

"Well ... but you don't know the script," Teacher Chen said. "Every time we've rehearsed the script you've struggled. There are a lot of words in mother bear's part, it's not at all easy."

"But she's learnt it," said Changxin.

"Truly?" Teacher Chen hesitated. "Who can guarantee it?"

Changxin, who was taking the part of the little bear, said that Aroma could because he and Hehuan had asked her to hear their lines, and she had memorized them better than Hehuan.

Teacher Chen made Aroma recite several passages and said, "Well, we'll just have to do it this way."

Changxin was delighted that Aroma would play the part of mother bear and was laughing all the time they were waiting for the play to start.

"What are you laughing at?" Aroma asked.

Changxin didn't say. He was an outstanding student and very quiet. Whenever he came across people fighting or something disappointing, he quietly avoided it because he did not care for it.

By contrast, Little Ox was standing there showing off. He shouted that he would only be happy to take the part of the hunter. He wanted the part of the bear least of all.

Aroma and Changxin went on stage and Changxin said, "How are you, Mum?"

Aroma said, "Good little boy."

The audience immediately burst into laughter because Changxin's mother was the head teacher. Everyone in the school knew this and now that they saw Aroma transformed into Changxin's mother they thought it very funny and laughed.

Little Ox was laughing and jeering.

Aroma felt awkward but tried hard not to let the interruptions affect her. It was the third day and she would be leaving soon, so she really tried to act well and not cause any problems, and to leave behind a good impression.

But Changxin was out of control among laughter. He was stammering on stage. The laughter increased. Little Ox was raising a rebellion.

Changxin was a gentle boy, tall with pale skin and bright eyes and a face that glowed with intelligence. Normally he was very clever and liked inventing things. He wrote elegant, good-looking characters but he just could not act. On stage his limbs froze and he was unhappy at being the target for ridicule, so the more he spoke the more he stammered and the more he stammered the more he spoke.

Everybody was having a great time. When Aroma heard Little Ox shouting "two stupid bears" she held back and didn't jump down from the stage to have it out with him.

The performance finished at last. Aroma was boiling with anger and Little Ox was delighted. He patted Changxin on the head and said, "Stupid bear." He patted Aroma on the head too, saying, "Stupid mother bear."

Aroma could stand it no longer and she started to quarrel with Little Ox.

Teacher Chen pulled them apart and looked at Little Ox with a frown. Little Ox said in a small voice, "I'm wrong, I'll do better next time."

Teacher Chen looked at Aroma who said, "I haven't done anything wrong."

Teacher Chen's fine eyebrows twitched and formed a knot in the middle.

"It was Little Ox who provoked me ..."

"So you don't intend to improve, is that it?" Teacher Chen said, her voice rising.

"When he's improved and doesn't provoke me anymore there won't be a problem," said Aroma.

"You're beginning to contradict your teacher," said Teacher Chen even more angrily.

"I'm not. I'm just saying that when he's improved and doesn't provoke me, then there will be no problem." At this point Aroma felt wronged and continued, "When I say there's no problem, then there's no problem, and in any case I won't be here tomorrow and won't have to share a desk with him ..."

"What? What?" Teacher Chen exclaimed. "What a child, you're really too much."

Teacher Chen had another class and so sent Aroma to the head teacher.

Waiting in the Head Teacher's Office

In Aroma's eyes, it was a pretty bad business. Having, with some difficulty, achieved her withdrawal from school tomorrow, here she was today in a mess.

Aroma knew the head teacher. She was Changxin's mother and lived in the Zhang Residence. Her home was not far from Aroma's home in the middle of Springwater Lane. Head Teacher Zhang went in and out of the same lane as Aroma and the others every day so she smiled at Aroma as if she were a sweet little girl, but at the time she had only recognized her face and didn't know that she was called Aroma. But now it was bad. Head Teacher Zhang had just seen her perform on the stage and it was under these circumstances that she now knew her name.

Starting of like this really embarrassed Aroma.

She walked slowly into the head teacher's office with head down and tears at the corner of her eyes, the very picture of dejection.

Head Teacher Zhang, perhaps recognizing Aroma as a familiar face, smiled and said, "Sit down."

She carried on working, now and then smiling at Aroma to indicate that she had not forgotten her.

To begin with, Aroma was very tense but later she slowly relaxed.

She felt that Head Teacher Zhang was very graceful. She was very good-looking with slightly arched almond eyes and a calm expression. She could even have been a fairy immortal descending to earth, but she was rather oddly dressed, not as simply as a fairy. What she was wearing today had a Chinese fan design on the front and Aroma remembered that in the winter she had worn an expensive overcoat with a fur collar which had caused a tremor in the neighborhood. Foxy Mum had said that the material for the overcoat was an all-wool velveteen fabric. When Foxy Dad had had money he had bought a similar coat for her. It was very smart and when she had entered a restaurant wearing it, everybody had rushed to open doors for her. Later, when Little Ox's elder brother had been born and there was no money for powdered milk or for the celebration of the baby's first month, the overcoat had been pawned and Foxy Dad had never had the money to redeem it.

Head Teacher Zhang was very busy with telephone calls all the time. While she was taking a telephone call she took a slip of paper and wrote on it: "The greatest lesson of all is the blessing of learning how to exist with other people," and pushed it towards Aroma.

Head Teacher Zhang finished her telephone call and finding Aroma's liquid dark eyes fixed on her, said, "You already know? Then go back to your classroom and carry on with your lessons."

"Truly?" Aroma asked. "Just like that?"

Head Teacher Zhang smiled and nodded.

Head Teacher Zhang nodded very elegantly and made Aroma feel that she had been treated courteously. Head Teacher Zhang had not treated her as somebody who should be punished but as a little girl who was an accidental visitor to the head teacher's office.

In fact, Head Teacher Zhang had said nothing that would cause embarrassment to anybody and Aroma had understood many truths. Such a good head teacher, it would be wonderful to be her daughter, to follow her and listen to her relaxed conversation. Aroma was willing. She could not let such a head teacher feel disappointed.

As she was thinking Aroma suddenly felt sad on her mother's behalf but from then on she was no longer afraid of school. She thought that Head Teacher Zhang was very good at talking and was very polite and understood children, so school was a good place.

The three days of Aroma's bet with her father had passed. On the morning of the fourth day he got everything ready in a low-key way and took Aroma to school as normal. On the way they met Hehuan and Dad told them to carry on to school together. Aroma wanted to talk to him about what had happened during the three days but said nothing. In any case, he had not talked it over with her either. Sometimes people in life set us puzzles. Let's try another three days, she thought.

The next three days passed swiftly. Let's try another three she thought. Anyhow, going to school is quite pleasant.

In the end, somehow unconsciously, even Aroma forgot about the basis of the concept of just going to school for three days.

My Father with a Heart of Stone

Worldly-Wise

When I was a child I lived with my mother and father in an old house on Nanchang Road. It had been built some time ago and was rather dilapidated but the imposing classical, square, public reception room was enormous and seemed, to the eye of a child, so wide that it was like a great palace. Outside there were two courtyards, one small one large, surrounded by high walls. There was a well in the smaller courtyard. Adjacent to this courtyard and surrounding the house was a garden filled to bursting with flowers and shrubs. The house had three stories and the staircase was so wide that four or five children could march up the stairs abreast. On each floor there were ten or more small rooms where a number of families lived.

Our family lived in the ground floor reception room. The neighbors said that the concubine of a big shot from the Shanghai Bund had originally occupied this room, and she had stashed a considerable amount of gold and jewelry here. One night, in troubled times, she had mysteriously fled without having the time to retrieve it. Perhaps the jewelry were still hidden somewhere in the room.

Was our home really the secret hiding place of jewelry? My mother and father and grandmother too had moved into the reception room and lived there for many years. We had never seen even the shadow of a hidden hoard of jewelry.

But there had been a burglar. He had searched far and wide and in places he had wrenched up the long floorboards. I don't know whether or not he had found the legendary hoard. But he was a burglar with a black heart and had made off with Granny's bluestone back-scratcher and an ancient watch.

Granny had become accustomed to these two objects through long use. She was heartbroken. As she nailed down the boards she whispered, "Why didn't the burglar behave decently when he took the risk of coming and stealing my treasured belongings?" continuing, "if he'd had a shred of conscience and had found the concubine's hoard, he'd have left a little so that I could have savored a new experience."

At the supper table that night Granny said that she thought that the concubine's hoard was probably not under the floorboards. Could it be in the fireplace? I listened and said, "Not so loud Granny. If you let the burglar know, he'll be back here again."

Dad laughed and said that I was worldly-wise.

The first time I heard the phrase "worldly-wise" I didn't know whether it was good or bad. But as I had been the subject of the comment I took it all in.

I was six at the time and basically understood what adults were saying ... but if there was a hidden meaning, I only half understood and took it at face value. However, most of the metaphors had nothing to do with me. I took no notice of them and like an insect blown past the ear on a puff of wind, did not think to investigate deeply.

Sometimes, when I was scolded by my mother and father and I felt that it was discouraging or unpleasant to listen to, I would pretend not to understand. This time, however, was an exception. I really did not understand whether my father was praising me or mocking me. After mulling it over for half a minute and still unable to guess, my brain suggested: is this a phrase that carries a mysterious meaning?

I was excited to be so closely associated with mystery and asked, "Dad, is worldly-wise ..."

"Don't talk nonsense at mealtimes," said Granny as she placed a fried egg in my bowl with her chopsticks and continued, "eat your egg and nourish your brain if you don't want to be a stupid child."

Granny was a power in the family and everybody deferred to her. This made her dictatorial and outspoken, there were no concessions to sentiment. Her cold gaze extinguished my inquisitive enthusiasm and I turned my face away and looked at the egg.

Granny had many skills. She had fried the egg beautifully so that it looked like a tiny straw hat. The edge of the white of the egg was crisply fried and slightly raised like a stiffened hat brim while the rest of the egg white had spread out with little raised bubbles of oil on its surface. As you took a mouthful it felt like soft, rippling silk, as if in ferment. The yellow of the egg was also as I liked it, and seven or eight parts hot. It was runny, with a sticky yolk and had not been overcooked. Overcooked egg yolks taste powdery to the tongue and lose their fresh delicacy. The egg before me was just beginning to congeal so that I had to swallow it in a mouthful, savoring it slowly. The soft round heart in the center of the yolk was particularly delicious.

I had always liked eggs. Not only was I enchanted by their taste, I also had a vague reverence for them.

Granny firmly believed that eating eggs made children intelligent. This function, in her hands, became a legend. She passed on her experience to friends and relatives and said that to start with I had been an utterly stupid child. The source of my present intelligence was the fact that since I had been born she had fed me an egg a day.

Granny's suggestion made me believe that eating eggs was the source of intelligence. If you did not eat eggs you would degenerate and quickly become a stupid child. In order to suppress fear and disorder I regarded the eating of eggs as a sacred task.

The satisfied expression on my face as I ate the egg attracted the attention of my father who expressed pleasure and said, "Children will be children. How lovable."

The "worldly wisdom" that I had quietly acquired seemed no bad thing ...

Every day from then on, I bade farewell to that inexperienced little girl. My sensibilities grew richer and I acquired an awareness of my own. These ideas sprang from my own mind. Perhaps, after all, I was "worldly-wise."

I discovered that my father had grown a heart of stone. The child he liked was not me but Wisteria. I hid this secret away in my heart and told nobody.

At that time, there was only one day off a week—Sunday. Every Sunday Dad took me to the home of a colleague to "play with Wisteria."

Wisteria's home was some distance away. My father walked fast and I always arrived panting and breathless.

Wisteria's home had a huge reception room with floor length windows that opened onto a terrace. A blustery wind blew in, making you feel that you were in the open.

Wisteria could play the piano, she could draw and she could recite. When she drew a mouse it looked like the real thing. In my eyes she could do everything. Moreover, she had an attractive face, a charming smile, a healthy body, a gentle character and when she saw Dad she greeted him sweetly ...

As for me, only my brain worked. I had a string of minor illnesses and I was as thin as a monkey but still wanted to play. When I went to see Wisteria I waited lifelessly for her to finish piano practice before we could play houses together.

When we played houses we liked to imitate the life of grown-ups. Wisteria played her fashionable mother to perfection and I played the part of an old toffee seller woman or a tough policewoman. If we played soldiers and bandits I played the evildoer with exceptional gusto. It seemed far more satisfying than playing good parts: no standing on ceremony and you could launch your attack when you wanted.

I didn't mind playing bandit parts but Wisteria wouldn't play bandits or evildoers. If you insisted she simply wouldn't play. She often played by herself. Because she had so many hobbies and so many little friends wanting to play with her, she seemed to be surrounded by a halo that drew people to her.

We also pretended to be doctors and nurses. At the time, I had no understanding of status and loved playing at active occupations, fighting to play the nurse and unwilling to be the doctor. A nurse was always busy, bandaging the injured, giving injections and feeding patients pills of bitter medicine. By contrast, Wisteria liked to be the doctor, sitting there seriously and using a stethoscope.

By the time we finished playing, Wisteria was as pretty as ever and I was covered in sweat. Dad said with approval that Wisteria's name was poetic. It was as good a name for a person as a flower. He also said that she was quiet and sensible.

I lowered my head. An insect seemed to gnaw at my heart, and I was hurt because I too thought that Wisteria was quite something. It was just that in my pursuit of her I would never achieve perfection.

However, I forgot my mood of unhappiness when we left Wisteria's home. Dad held my hand tightly and listened to whatever childish song I sang along the way, as if he were listening to Wisteria playing a popular tune, something he never did with Wisteria herself.

Gradually, I became used to listening attentively to Wisteria practicing the piano. Gradually too, I became familiar with the world's popular tunes. Beyond that there was an indistinct realization in my heart of the sort of child that my father preferred.

Later, as I slowly grew up, I came to see that the expectations of a girl were very different to those of a sweaty little boy. A girl's ability to maintain her beauty and elegance was something to be appreciated and taken seriously. Wisteria had been like that since she was born.

The Alarm Clock that Sounded Ten Thousand Times

My father loved gardening. He got up on time every morning, donned his straw hat and went into the garden to weed, to water busily and to graft stems. He had his own spade, watering can, saw and insect spray. Those who did not know might have mistaken him for a laborer.

In the garden behind the house he had planted loquats, pomegranates, canna lilies and sunflowers. With me he had planted a castor oil plant and a loofah, both carefully tended.

There were also his treasured bonsai pots, moved outside in fine weather and brought into the reception room, one by one, when there was a gale or rainstorm. Every winter the scent of the narcissus plants he had grown assailed the nostrils, and the kumquats glistened crystal bright with yellow and produced tiny fruit like little lamps, or, even more, like bead upon bead of yellow topaz.

There was a galvanized iron watering can by the kumquat tree. I used it sometimes for watering. It was very heavy and required all my strength as I grunted to lift it. Dad once said that the sound of flowers opening was wonderful. It was the sound of nature. Because of my father's influence I loved flowers. I would creep into the garden and sit by a plant that was about to blossom, quietly waiting for the flower to emerge from its bud.

Unfortunately, the flower upon which I had set my heart was slow to bloom. Like a reticent bride it hesitated and dithered, seemingly wishing to grow by itself unseen, unwilling for people to catch sight of how it blossomed.

I often thought: is it only butterflies and bees that can hear the sound of a flower blossoming? But my father had watched flowers open with his own eyes and said, "Some flowers open silently at night, some open early in the morning. Flowers do not like being disturbed, if you want to watch them opening you must be calm in your heart."

I really wanted to still my heart and then sit quietly by a flower but there were too many things that attracted my gaze. There were times when I would turn away and the flower would open in a flash. But this didn't upset me. Flowers without number grew in the garden. Flowers blossomed every year and at every season. They had never failed to produce beautiful blooms on time. Therefore, one should be happy.

Children have a kind of enchanting temperament, as radiant as sunshine. Every morning I loved to linger in the garden, even if there were no flowers going to open. There was a lacquered dovecote the color of a postbox in a corner beyond the garden. I would stand there in a dream wondering what it would feel like if it suddenly started to rain and I hid in there like a dove, calmly waiting for the rain to stop.

I liked the local Yandang kindergarten. It was very well known and hidden away in a little alley as long and narrow as a writing brush pot. The head was a kind, chubby, grandmotherly woman who would greet the children at the entrance as they arrived for school.

Sometimes, when I thought that I would see the smiling face of the grandmotherly head, I would put all my strength into running and would run and run and then see an unnamed wild flower at the roadside and think, "Is this the latest flower?" I would stop despite myself, consider it minutely and smell it: it could be no bad thing to be the first child to smell its scent. Unconsciously, I lingered for a while and by the time I reached the kindergarten the narrow little alley was completely empty and the grandmotherly head was nowhere to be seen. Everybody had already gone in.

Sometimes my father, seeing that it was almost time, would urge me off to the kindergarten without delay. I trotted past Fuxing Park and couldn't help taking a look at the locksmith making keys or gazing at the hawker selling rice wine or the assistant who was frying several fat dough twists. By the time I had regained my senses and flown headlong into the alley my heart sank: how could I have been late again?

My father knew that I was often late because Granny Head raised the matter. The next day Dad secretly followed me. He saw that I left on time, that I browsed by the wayside and that I couldn't take a direct route to my objective. Even when it was time I didn't rush to the kindergarten. This made my father sigh.

It was because he had been a soldier. He got up, planted flowers and went to work as accurately as clockwork. He breakfasted in a hurry and even the leisurely evening meal seemed to occupy a set time and he gobbled down his food inside fifteen minutes or so. It didn't matter whether it was an ordinary day or a holiday, or whether my uncle and other guests were there. He finished eating on time. However, he always politely remained at the table with the guests after finishing, slowly sipping a cup of tea.

Time after time I was late and my father became extremely concerned. He said that being late could lead to delays and leave people with a bad impression. A child who was heedless, who did not keep to time, would in the long run become slack because the uneasiness and guilt at being late could make them frustrated and unhappy.

He explained the logic to me over and over again. I was sad in myself and wrote "being late" on a strip of paper and then dug a hole in the garden and buried it. I said a funeral service over it which included the words: "Don't look for me, 'being late.'"

At that moment, I felt that I had said goodbye forever to the bad habit of being late.

I was not late for the next two days and I gradually calmed down and felt that "being late" had really been buried.

Having been to "play with Wisteria" on Sunday and on my way to kindergarten on Monday I discovered a small beetle with a hard shell on the branch of a tree. His shell was the color of gold and shone in the outside light.

I stretched out a hand thinking to feel its thick shell. It felt it and drew away, climbing up and up until suddenly it fell. I said, "What kind of insect are you, is your shell too heavy?"

I was forced to wonder: what insect is this, why have I never seen it before? Can a little insect dressed in shining armor feel pride?

The little insect didn't speak and in slow silence laboriously took off, its stubby wings beating with heavy effort as it flew. I pitied the little thing. It must have been its heavy gleaming shell that made flight so exhausting and ponderous. Is such a handsome shell a cause for joy or sadness?

Standing and looking at this strange insect made me late again.

Facing the anxious expression of Granny Head I thought: there are so many strange trees, plants and insects in the world, there are people with completely different faces and people live all kinds of secret lives. Shouldn't we look at it all a little more? Perhaps there is no way to bury being late.

Dad asked the reason for my being late. I told him the truth. He said nothing as he watched my spirited description of the unidentified insect, only, "There's nothing wrong with liking all this but you mustn't be late. If there's no magic in the world that will alter your original nature it would be better just not to be late."

Then something very strange happened. I still left at the same time and still watched the peddlers doing business on the streets. I still watched the dogs running about and people in uniform marching solemnly into the distance until they disappeared from sight, but I always met Granny Head smiling at the kindergarten entrance as she said, "Good morning child, have a good day!"

I was delighted. I had arrived very early on the second and third days and had discovered that there was an advantage to arriving early at kindergarten: I could chat with Granny Head and once she even gave me a sweet.

There were several occasions when it was utterly peaceful inside the kindergarten, which seemed to have been transformed into somewhere incomparably new.

I stood in front of the teacher's desk facing an array of small empty chairs and sang. The sound of my unrestrained singing was much better than normal. I sang several songs at the top of my voice to the listening chairs and felt myself quite a person.

More often than not I played in the inner courtyard of the kindergarten and found joy beyond measure amongst the shrubs, wild flowers and bamboo that decorated it. One day, under the dripping eaves, I found a shape formed by a water splash that looked like a palace of extraordinary design built like a fortress. The splashes alongside looked like the cut out silhouettes of streets and parks. But by the time my little companions arrived the fairytale palace had disappeared as the water slowly dried out. I told my little friends that I had seen the finest and rarest water splash of all.

I gradually became used to not being late anymore. But just when I felt that I must have been receiving some magical help, my mother told me the secret. The clocks in our house were ten minutes faster than everybody else's.

Dad had approved of the fact that I watched the silversmith at work and talked to the birds in the trees and that there were so many things to be involved in although I didn't want to be late. So he secretly advanced all the clocks and watches by ten minutes.

Year by year, throughout my childhood, the alarm clock sounded "not on time" a myriad times, each time ten minutes early. I became used to this accelerated time and everything was more relaxed.

It allowed me to avoid panic and brought tranquility, and because I didn't have a guilty conscience about being late it freed me from anger as well.

The sound of those myriad early alarms slowly allowed me to taste the joy of being on time. Sometimes, when I looked at the scurrying children beside me I sensed it was because they had not found the joy of "extra time." They did not have a father like mine, or inaccurate alarm clocks.

A Story at the Tip of My Tongue

My grandmother came from Ningbo in Zhejiang Province. When she was young she had come to Shanghai in the company of her grandfather who was in the shipping business. She had never returned to Ningbo. Though she had lived in Shanghai all those years she still spoke with a proper Ningbo accent. The dishes she cooked every day and the snacks she prepared were all Ningbo style. Her friends were mostly people from Ningbo, and her lifestyle and tastes and her obstinate appetite all made it seem that she had grown a heart from Ningbo.

I grew up on my grandmother's Ningbo cooking. My stomach and tastes were all on the one side, the Ningbo side. I understood every word of my grandmother's Ningbo dialect and loved to do exaggerated imitations of it. However, there was a generation between us and though my grandmother was kind, I was more emotionally attached to my mother, and I looked like her as well.

My mother was accustomed to Ningbo food but her taste was broad. She liked Shanghai and Cantonese cuisine, and even western food became a favorite. She had been born in Shanghai and spoke a pure Shanghai dialect. When she was talking with my father their speech was often filled with "our Shanghai" type phrases, redolent of the heavy superiority born of being Shanghainese.

I took after my mother and considered myself Shanghainese, not out of personal vanity but out of a sincere attachment to the city, a love of Huaihai Road near our home and its shops, and most of all its food shops and bookstalls. I loved to walk through the New City God's Temple of Shanghai to see a film at the Grand Theater. After the cinema there was another programme: gazing with stretched neck up at the twenty-four stories of the Shanghai Park Hotel.

I loved the pig-tailed trams clanging majestically forward. They turned corners like wounded snakes, writhing in embarrassment as they did so.

I remember that at the time there was also a kind of bus with a large black rubber sack on top that blew up into a huge bag. It was said to be a methane vehicle and from a distance it looked like the soft mat used in physical training lessons. Perhaps methane gas was heavy? When the bus started up it seemed top-heavy and juddered the whole time like a strange great frog, giving me countless odd fantasies.

Shanghai was where I lived. At the time, I had never been anywhere apart from Shanghai and my vague love for all the tribes of the world was fixed on Shanghai. I couldn't imagine how, in other places, they opened the curtains on life every day. Were people kind in other places? Were the dark nights particularly long in other places?

Because of locality, there were continuous little domestic irritations. My grandmother couldn't understand mandarin and my father couldn't understand the Ningbo dialect. It was very funny when they wanted to exchange views. They always tried to guess what the other was saying and if they guessed correctly all was well. Sometimes they gestured to each other, guessing wildly like a cow's head to a horse's mouth, and only if it was really unintelligible would they ask my mother or me to translate.

Fortunately they both understood Shanghai dialect though they couldn't speak it and it became our "official language." Both sides were content when I used Shanghai dialect to interpret for them.

My father attempted to avoid the embarrassment of having to use an interpreter at home by learning the Shanghai dialect with me so as to ease communication with my grandmother. However, he had no gift for the language, his tongue couldn't get round the words and he had a fatal weakness: he was very thin skinned. He was ashamed to seek instruction from his own daughter and so learned very tentatively.

After practicing for a while my father summoned up his courage and spoke in his Shanghai dialect to my grandmother, but she didn't understand. He tried harder but to my grandmother it was still like having her head in a fog.

From then on my father simply gave up learning the Shanghai dialect and even abandoned all that he had learned already.

My grandmother had always regarded my father as an outsider, a northerner. Despite this she had accepted him and praised him as being the most even-tempered of her three sons-in-law.

My mother liked to joke with my father. She joked about his outlandish accent, his lack of sophistication and his frugality but she treasured him and she always kept him back a portion of whatever delicacies my grandmother had cooked while he was out.

My father came from a hill village near Yimeng in Shandong Province. In his teens he had joined the army where he had met my mother. He had been in his late twenties and she was seven years younger. For her sake he had changed occupations and stayed in Shanghai.

My father was the head of the family but his northern habits had no effect upon the course of family life.

My mother controlled the family finances. The family furniture, furnishings and daily essentials were bought according to her preferences. The drapes over the windows and the bed curtains were plain but elegant and not unfashionable. They had a western air and reflected my mother's aesthetic tastes.

The family furnishings, it could be seen plainly, were Shanghai style and Grandma ruled "matters of tongue and taste". She cooked Ningbo cuisine at home every day. This household actually belonged to the south.

The ingredients most used in Grandma's Ningbo cooking were eggs and pickles together with fish and prawns from river and sea, as well as all kinds of shellfish. Dad did not much care for fish and prawns. Perhaps he felt that spitting out the fish bones was too much trouble and that spitting out the shells of prawns somehow detracted from his military image.

Dad inclined much more to wheat-based food and to meat. If the two could be combined that suited his taste even more. At New Year and other festivals he would make a sort of ravioli called *jiaozi* stuffed with everything from rice to vegetables. The way he ate them was also different from the rest of the family. He would pour soya sauce, vinegar and sesame oil into a dish with some chili powder and a little garlic, dip the *jiaozi* into this seasoning, turn them several times until they were a bright red, and then eat them with relish.

Sometimes he made noodles. He liked to fill a bowl with steaming noodles, add pickles and shredded pork and then pour in some chili oil. Sometimes my mother would make him steamed buns. He would happily take one, bite it open and insert two dried chilies bought from the Native Produce Store saying, "Mmm ... not bad," as he gobbled it down in record speed.

I was not the same as my father. I disliked meat and noodles and preferred rice. I would eat fish and peel prawns with fascination and in order to enjoy the delicacies of seafood would spend a long time eating at the dining table.

Dad said I was like a cat, "I'd really like to take you home with me. The food at home is the most delicious of all. It's an addiction, food for the mind and the stomach, once eaten never forgotten."

Why was my unfathomable father talking this way? "Home"

was a place that I had never visited. What I knew of it lingered on paper only. For example, letter after letter postmarked in red with my father's name on them.

In the autumn, at harvest time, there were parcels from home too. Each time the postman delivered a parcel slip it had to be stamped with my father's personal seal. The slip always bore my father's name and nobody else's seal could be used. This made me feel that home belonged to my father alone.

I don't know how many times my father had told me that he missed the food at home. In his memory, the millet pancakes, fennel *jiaozi*, fried radish dumplings and chicken stewed in aubergines were superior even to the food of the immortals.

I gradually came to remember that list of dishes whilst, at the same time, the name "home" lodged in my mind. It was a distant place that I had yet to encounter but it was connected to me at every moment.

Perhaps there were dim memories of home. I gradually took notice of the parcels that came from there. They were all wrapped in coarsely stitched, earth colored material. They bulged with shelled peanuts and my grandmother used to remove the red outer skins to make a fragrant dish of peanuts with kelp.

Home also dispatched dates that my grandmother steamed, dried in the sun and then soaked in Shaoxing rice wine. In taste they had a honey sweetness tinged with alcohol. Once, strangely, my distant grandfather sent two large succulent melons and a bag of huge, sweet potatoes by the hand of a distant relative who was being posted to Shanghai in the army. Grandfather said that he had grown them himself.

Home Rediscovered

Winter passed, then spring and as late spring approached my parents talked about taking me on a trip.

My mother brandished a map in a flurry of searching. It became her constant companion. She took it everywhere. Whenever there was a spare moment she examined it absorbedly as if it was the finest picture on earth, saying, "The world's large, I'd really like to take a trip round it to look at the most beautiful scenery."

Dad asked me where I wanted to go and I replied that I wanted to go anywhere where flowers blossomed: where they blossomed year on year, month by month and day by day.

"Good, good," my father nodded.

Mum said that nothing was as good as a place of picturesque scenery with hills and water where you could sunbathe on the hillside during the day, look at the white-topped waves on the sea in the afternoon, and dream under the stars at night.

"Come with me," said Dad, "and there'll be no need to go looking for beautiful scenery on a map, it's here in my heart."

Dad bought the train tickets and took us to his home in Yimeng. "This is your husband's and daughter's home," he said to my mother, "best give in to the majority."

Listening to my father saying so definitely that this was my home, I wondered, could it be that this was indeed my home?

But it was a place that I had never visited before. It was completely strange.

My father made an obeisance to the distant Yimeng Mountain and pointing to the two trees at the entrance to the village said, "I planted those when I was young. Quickly, come and look at the trees I planted when I was a boy."

The pica birds in the trees started to call, as if answering him.

At home, I met grandfather. He lived in an old house where the courtyard was hung about with red lanterns. Grandfather had been born there, and so had his grandfather before him. The courtyard was large, there were no obstructions in front and you could see the wide-open fields. Standing in the courtyard and looking out there really were flowers blossoming on the paths that ran between the fields. The earth was covered in green vegetables and farm crops. You could also see, moving forward from the distance, a crowd of people dressed in farming clothes.

They did not disappear from sight because they were relatives, coming to grandfather's house to visit Dad.

Fellow villagers also came visiting, amongst them a large fat granny who swayed as she walked and had difficulty in standing. Grandfather gave her a chair to sit in. Perhaps she was the fattest person in the village? The moment she sat down she was imprisoned by the two arms of the chair like somebody who had grown into an armchair. Standing at her knee was a thin dark girl of about my age. Frightened of strangers, she tried to squeeze in between Fat Granny's legs. She was called Precious Chrysanthemum.

Precious Chrysanthemum's father was mining coal a thousand miles away and her mother had gone to look after him. All that remained of the family were Precious Chrysanthemum, the two old people, grandfather and Fat Granny, and a big black dog.

In a while the postman came calling. He knew everybody in the village and said that Precious Chrysanthemum's dad had sent money. Her grandfather was delighted, his mouth opening to expose yellowing teeth. He trembled with excitement, his eyes reddened and his nose nearly started to run as he reached his right index finger to the red ink paste, dipped it in, withdrew it, and pressed his fingerprint on the receipt.

He thrust the money into an inner pocket, covering it with his hand and repeatedly pressing it down. I asked my father, "Is this old grandfather a money-grubbing devil?"

"That's life-saving money," my father told me. "Starvation apart, sickness used to be the lifelong companion of the poor. Starvation has been solved but the unfortunate can still become caught up in sickness. More than anything, the poor are frightened of falling ill. Precious Chrysanthemum's granny is seriously ill with oedema. If you press her anywhere it leaves a hollow. The money that her father sends is for her medical treatment."

I looked at Precious Chrysanthemum's granny and she smiled serenely back at me. I felt a little like crying.

Dinner for all was from the same pot, cooked over firewood in an iron dish.

Dad kept back his visiting relatives for the meal. The younger wives of the family had already brought delicious steamed bread, millet pancakes, fennel *jiaozi*, fried radish dumplings, chicken in aubergine stew, meat patties and salted bean curd. My father had bought the Co-Operative Store out of tinned meat, candy, alcohol and cigarettes.

The cabbage with meat stew was served in a large metal washbasin. The meat included fatty strips cut thick and there was carp and scrambled egg together with the wild mushrooms, fruit, goat's milk and chestnuts provided by village relatives, in all a feast for hundreds. I had never imagined such a riotous banquet.

The courtyard was filled with children scampering about. Some were prattling their first words and there was one who choked because of eating and drinking too fiercely and who cried when teased by his parents. Several mongrel dogs darted in and out of the press of people looking for scraps.

Amidst all this hubbub I was proud: I would never be alone, even in the distant hills there would still be so many relations. They regarded our arrival as a festival. My feelings for home had not become more and more distant but, rather, accepting of all of this. The home that had existed on paper had changed its appearance because of living people and their emotions.

Once having eaten, Precious Chrysanthemum lost her timidity and pulled me away to talk, taking me to the bank of the stream. This quick-witted, deft little girl made a clay doll and gave it to me. All the little companions seemed to be able to do the same. They made clay dolls and set them in front of me, all arguing that the doll they had made themselves was the best looking. Nor could they be persuaded otherwise: they all hoped to gain face in front of a guest.

Precious Chrysanthemum and I became good friends and led the daily life of mischievous village children. We didn't want to do the same thing every day, herding goats in the morning and picking wild fruit in the afternoon. On the second day we went to market with grandfather and each day we thought together how we could live a bright, glorious and fragrant life.

Precious Chrysanthemum enjoyed running around in the open and catching grasshoppers. She also knew every animal in the area as well as all sorts of trees and plants. This landscape was ancient and so much had grown there and there was more to come.

I discovered that in this little world Precious Chrysanthemum could do everything and knew everything. When we were together she was always lively, resolute and friendly.

It was my aunt that my father was most concerned about. She was his elder sister. My grandmother had died when Dad was a baby and while grandfather was away working in the Northeast my aunt had looked after this child deprived of its mother's love. Brother and sister relied upon each other throughout their lives.

When Dad enlisted, my aunt was desolated. She struck him and wept all day but in the end she couldn't hold him back and he escaped.

She married not long after he left. I've seen the wedding photograph. She was very good-looking then. Her husband had a little medical knowledge and was well able to get by. But the son she bore him was handicapped and other misfortunes followed so that the eager young wife was heartbroken. She felt oppressed and no longer wished to live. She clawed at her own face, tried to strangle herself with a rope and collapsed on the ground. She was resuscitated but always suffered from depression.

The tonic medicine that Dad brought home with him was mostly for his sister. When I met her I saw that she was old and bent. Filled with despair, she wept tremulously when she saw Dad. I felt my aunt was in distress, a person without hope.

My aunt wept and wept and in a daze flailed at my father with her fists.

My father accepted the blows in silent misery. He said that she hadn't hurt him, she was old and weak and in no state to injure him. This was my father's most heartrending moment.

Seeing my stonehearted father so unexpectedly hurt, I wept and my aunt wept too, it seemed in remorse.

My father dried our tears, saying, "Don't cry, crying makes you ugly."

Every morning during those few days my father went walking by himself in the depths of the countryside and would sit in the sun, frowning in dejection.

I asked my mother why Dad was so sad.

My mother said that my father had been devastated by what had happened to his sister. My father's mother had died not long after he was born and he had grown up on the "collective milk" of relatives and neighbors. My grandfather had subsequently married again. His new wife had loved my father dearly and he had transferred his love for his mother to her. However, his stepmother did not get on with his sister who loved only her younger brother. She had stood by him when he was young and had not left him for a moment. When she saw him well, a sweet smile appeared on her face but later because life did not go smoothly she lost all joy, her face grew long and her eyes were dark with suffering.

Dad loved his elder sister and her misfortunes troubled him deeply. Returning from his walk he told me quietly, "Your aunt is kind-hearted, intelligent and spirited but small-minded and hot-tempered. She cannot stand it when things don't go her way, which is why everything fell to pieces. Like your aunt, you are quick-witted and ambitious and similar in temperament. I like that. But you must be strong and open-hearted and not go the way of your aunt."

I said, "I won't, I want to be a happy child."

Dad said, "But you will grow up and when you do, a lot of good things will have gone. You won't be able to cry when you want to, or laugh when you want to. But you must get over it and make yourself happy. One can always be enriched."

Ever since I was small my father had always wanted me to be steady minded and perceptive. This was because he was afraid that fate and heredity might operate between my aunt and myself. Most of all he was afraid that I might become like my aunt: bigoted, unhappy and only able to see the thorns in life.

He said, "Child, remember you must be bright and big-hearted. That's the way to seize happiness. Happiness is fleeting and dies easily."

On the morning of the day we left, Precious Chrysanthemum came and clasped little fingers with me, swearing an oath that we would never forget our friendship.

My aunt also came to see us off, looking tragic and not speaking, like a beetle concealed beneath its shell.

My father put on a smiling face and talked expansively about his childhood, about the time he had been scolded by my aunt for dressing up as a bandit and about the first time he had caught a pheasant in the woods and how proud she had been. All this had been decades ago but they both remembered.

My father said, "I'd really like to be back then."

I said in agitation, "Dad, why don't you think of me? If you're a child again won't I not be here?"

My father said, "I can't go back. It's just that I miss the hills that raised me and the relatives that brought me up, and the person I was: brave, with no wish for a conventional life and with no worries. When I think of me as I was, I seem to acquire a strength difficult to describe and I don't then look down my nose at who I was when I was young."

The train arrived. I was overjoyed. We were going home and I felt that the train was sweetness itself. It was only when I thought of leaving Precious Chrysanthemum that I felt a little reluctance.

My aunt was different: she wept at the train.

My father, that rolling stone with his stranger's heart, was leaving his home further and further behind. He was sunk in gloom for a long while and perhaps for him, the train journey was tinged with a special sadness, like tears.

The Very First Secret

There were many children of the same age in the large building we lived in. There were some tearaway naughty boys that I didn't like and a few boys who were as gentle as girls. I called them "milksops" and rather looked down on them. Amongst the girls, the bigger ones would seek out slightly older girls to play with. When we were together they would frighten us with talk about bogeymen, demons or horror stories like *The Embroidered Slipper*. As a result it was only Little Swallow and a few others that were on good terms with me.

Little Banana was the closest to me. It only needed for Dad not to take me to "play with Wisteria" for her to appear at the door of her own accord and take me off to an isolated spot to talk, play houses and tell each other stories. She said, "I don't want to play with Little Swallow and the others. I want it to be just us two."

Little Banana's family kept goldfish. There was a large one she liked and she had given it the codename Shark. Her father was in charge of everything to do with the goldfish. He looked like a sumo wrestler, huge in girth, the very symbol of strength.

Little Banana was of a different style. She was small and dumpy with attractive curling eyelashes and a little mouth that liked to talk and to comment. She was never idle. She appeared good-natured but she was actually very temperamental, happy one moment and miserable the next.

I told Little Banana about our country home and Precious Chrysanthemum, and showed her the clay doll she had given me. She said, "I don't like Little Chrysanthemum."

"Why? You've never met her."

"She makes clay dolls, her hands will be very dirty."

"Little Chrysanthemum makes a doll and washes her hands in the stream and in a little while they are white and she can scoop fish from the stream too," I said.

Little Banana went on, "I'm not happy. When you're not there people are nasty to me and bully me."

I said, "You have this awesome father, other children won't dare cross you."

"It's my mother. She's horrible to Shark. She can't bear to see him snatching food and can't bear the fact that I like him. Tell me, do your mother and father like you?" asked Little Banana.

I didn't know what to say. I could only reply truthfully, "Sometimes Dad likes me, sometimes he doesn't but Mum likes me."

Little Banana said, "I'm the opposite of you. My father likes me but my mother doesn't."

"Why doesn't your mum like you?" I asked.

"It's a secret."

Little Banana boasted that she had a lot of secrets, like a whole string of fruit that could be picked in abundance whenever she wanted. She said secrets were things that other people didn't know and couldn't guess at. There were good secrets and there were bad secrets.

I said that I didn't have any secrets. Little Banana said, "I'll give you one, OK?"

"OK." I had thought that I would only have a secret when I was grown up but having one in advance wasn't bad.

Little Banana said, "I'm telling you, Mum and Dad may not be related to me. I hear a lot of children are adopted."

I was dumbfounded. There were three in Little Banana's family, all different. The neighbors would mock them saying that Little Banana, "Doesn't look like Mum or Dad but looks like the cobbler's lad."

Little Banana's mother was slim and delicate and spoke a soft Wu dialect. She was polite, reserved but rather over-courteous.

She was also over-attentive. Little Banana had only to invite me home and she would come and sit with us so that we were deprived of the freedom to play by ourselves. Worst of all, she kept on urging me to eat sweets and would unwrap them and stuff them in my mouth with her own hand.

At the time my teeth were growing and I often had toothache but, too embarrassed to refuse I just swallowed the sweets. The result was that Little Banana's mum was always stuffing sweets in my mouth so that I was forced to flee. Even now, whenever I think of her I get an uncomfortable, sweet, sticky sensation in my throat.

I took my concerns to mother and asked her, "Mum, you once said that I had been picked up somewhere. Why did you say that?"

Mum laughed and said, "What's so strange about that? When I was small your granny said the same thing about me."

Granny heard and chuckled, "Ah, all the children in this

building were found in dustbins, so you must be good otherwise you'll go back to the dustbin."

I was sensitive then and although it was late spring I still felt the cold, and when I washed my hands in cold water I would put my lips to my hands and blow warm breathe on them. After I had learned this first secret of all, and heard what my grandmother said, I was filled with anxiety but couldn't quite say why.

Thereafter I often had terrifying dreams, as if I had been tossed into an unfathomable black pit. I would wake in tears, and I dreamt that because I had been ruined I was not the child of my mother and father.

I was always thinking: who are my real mother and father? I hoped they were grand—emperor and empress of some distant land would be good—and that one day they would receive me into their palace. If they weren't quite so grand I hoped they'd be respectable. When I saw women quarrelling with people on the street, or women making a row outside the tobacconist's, the sound of their talking and cracking of melon seeds disgusted me. At the Nanchang Road crossroads there were some houses that opened on to the street where, at night, the men and women put out tables at the roadside and ate and drank alcohol. When the men had eaten and drunk their fill they would boast and curse all and sundry. When I saw them my scalp would tingle as if somebody had gripped me by the hair and I thought, "Please don't let these people be my real mother and father."

After a while, my father bought some new brushes and exercise books and made me practice writing characters.

I had to practice writing in the squares: large, small, many, few, up, down, come, go.

But I liked to draw pictures most of all. I would write characters in the book for a while and then draw pictures of fairies and clouds, stars and crowns.

My father saw them and said, "The next exercise book I buy for you, you must use for practicing characters. Characters are like a second face that embodies a person's cultivation. Do you understand?"

My father also, his hand on mine, taught me how to write the character *yong* (永), "eternal." He said that of all the characters in the language it was the most difficult to write.

I wrote a lot of the *yong* character but was not pleased. At the time I didn't understand why people required a "second face." I said, "I don't want one, don't want it, I want just one face and that's enough!"

My father scolded me. I felt wronged and the words in my heart burst out, "I don't want a stone-hearted father. I want to find my real mother and father."

My father asked, "You shouldn't have this weight on your mind. Tell me, where would you go to find them?"

"I want to go far away to find them but I'm too little so I need you and Mum to go with me to find them together." As I spoke I realized that the Mum and Dad I had would become strangers and I burst into tears.

"If you take us then you won't need to look for your mother and father. We are your real mother and father."

I couldn't help but reveal the secret. Dad roared with laughter and very soon everybody around knew of Little Banana's and my secret. But nobody took it seriously. They just laughed uproariously.

At first, when Little Banana found that I had told the secret she was furious and called me a traitor. But she soon forget and because we were close friends and mutually supportive, though there might sometimes be hard words and friction between us, we soon returned to harmony. Because the hearts of the young are resilient there are no deep wounds.

One day, Little Banana's mother, seeing Shark snatching food, scooped the unbearable fish out in a fury and dumped him on the table, intending to put him back shortly. But she forgot and Shark died.

Little Banana burst into tears and rushed over to our home, saying that she was going to look for her real parents and wasn't going to live with her wicked stepmother anymore.

Little Banana's mother cried as well, even more hurt than Little Banana ...

In the end, my mother appeared and made Little Banana go home, telling her that with her own eyes she had seen her mother pregnant with Little Banana and give birth to her.

After tormenting me for a while, my first secret was soon forgotten. In fact, why should you have to have secrets anyhow?

At the time, I wanted something just for myself, as evidence of my identity. However, my father had not scolded me and said that he had consulted a professor of child psychology who said that children required psychological danger so that they could overcome fear through this experience. A great many children experienced this sort of suspicion and there was nothing wrong with thoughts like these. In adults it would not be so ordinary.

Later my father said to me seriously, "You can play with Little Banana but you must remember that, although you can fantasize and play about, you must be cheerful. That's the only right way. I don't want you moping."

My father took me to play with Wisteria more often. He said that if I was like Wisteria, with a halo of talent and tolerance, I would be more approachable to people and would make more and better friends and would grow up better.

A Revelation of Life

My father was an expert in solitude. He could stay by himself in the garden for ages. Even on holidays there were times when he made no preparations or plans but just took life as it came.

There were times when, after lunch, he would suddenly have an idea and take me to see a film at the Grand Theatre. I was a great fan of films. Watching them was like being in a beautiful dream.

Dad wrote home every month and sent money. There was not much spare cash so he never ate out with me. However, he bought cinema tickets without hesitation but in all other respects he was very economical.

From where we lived on Nanchang Road it was four stops

to the Grand Theater, though Dad and I often walked through the New City God's Temple thus saving the bus fare. Each time we went on foot he would use the money saved from the bus fare to buy me popsicles and ice creams. In winter he would buy me sugar coated fruit on a stick or a firecracker.

One day, wearing my hair in a butterfly ribbon and dressed in a skirt and shoes, I went with Dad to the cinema but at the entrance somebody trod on my foot so painfully that I cried out.

My father reasoned with the man who trod on my foot and said, "You can go. I believe it wasn't deliberate but don't walk so recklessly in the future."

At the cinema my father lovingly massaged my swollen foot. Just that once he was exceptionally generous and after the film bought me a White Snow ice cream bar to make up for it.

I respected my father for the way that he did not lose his composure or courtesy under any circumstances.

When we went to bookshops my father spent generously and bought two copies of the same book, one for me and one to give to Wisteria.

My father made me read along with Wisteria. He said that Wisteria's description of people and events, hitherto unconnected, were very clear.

I did not intend to lag behind Wisteria, so when she read I read too. When she told a story from the book, I told two stories and in this way we both rapidly made great strides.

I would soon be going to school.

The person I was then had a head of soft and yellowish hair and paid great attention to the good things that other little girls of the same age might have. For example, Wisteria wore a pale green butterfly bow in her hair. It was not long before I had induced my mother to buy a pair for me.

Little Banana's mother bought her a brand new red school satchel. It was gorgeous. I looked at it and my heart trembled.

Remembering that the autumn weather was dry, my heart was ensnared by this red satchel. Everything else retreated into the distance. I even felt that happy or not I was inextricably linked to the red satchel. All the more so since every day Little Banana proclaimed in my ear how beautiful and useful her satchel was. A single thought formed in my head: I definitely must have a satchel like that as well.

For several days in a row I searched the streets and found just such a satchel in a small stationery shop. Separated by a pane of gleaming glass I discovered that it was even more attractive. I stood before it for a long time, looking at it up close and then from a distance, then, later, covering one eye and looking with the other.

"There's nothing that can compare with it in beauty, truly," I thought at the time.

In the evening I rushed to the tram stop and waited for three trams until my mother got off one. She looked at me in astonishment. I said nothing and seizing her hand, dragged her to the stationery shop where I pointed to the red satchel and said, "Buy it for me, please, Mum."

"But Dad has bought you a new satchel. It's quite nice too."

At a loss, I wanted to cry. Mum stroked my head and her heart softened. When she produced her purse to pay she found that she didn't have enough money. At that moment the shop closed.

At night I dreamed—dreamed that somebody had cut up the red satchel in the shop with a large pair of scissors. I was so agitated that I shouted out. Dad woke me and said quietly, "Why be like this? Whatever satchel you use has nothing to do with whether you are happy or not."

"It does," I said, "without it, I'm unhappy."

"Then I'll lay a bet with you that, without it, you'll be as happy as usual."

Dad had no intention of buying it for me and I was naturally displeased and blamed him for his heart of stone, but the displeasure, like bad weather, soon passed.

In the spring of the following year, on my birthday, Dad came home pushing his bicycle and holding high the red satchel.

I snatched the red satchel and whirled happily round the room with it.

It was only after my bout of happiness that I saw that Mum was rubbing Dad with turpentine ointment. In order to get to the shop faster Dad had taken his bicycle and had collided with a delivery trishaw. A large swelling had appeared on his knee.

My heart sank: how had I fallen for this red satchel to the exclusion of all else and how had I not seen that my father had injured his knee because of it?

My father said, "There's nothing wrong with love of beauty but there are lots of good things in life. If you trail behind others you'll never catch up."

True, Little Banana had recently changed her satchel for a new one. It was green and she said that a green-colored satchel was well worth a second look.

The red satchel eventually wore out but I treasured it as if it was a baby, if not for anything else, then for what my father had said. It may not have been easy listening but it was a revelation of life.

The Person My Father Believed in Most of All

I was a difficult child when I was growing up and would often think of all sorts of things: such as, if everything was turned upside down and the grown-ups listened to the children, what sort of place would the world be?

My father quickly gave me an accurate answer.

Once, when I was in the garden waiting for flowers to blossom I saw that a sunflower planted in the garden could dance—when the sun rose I discovered that it was swaying elegantly to and fro.

I told Little Banana of this discovery. She didn't believe it and told some of her fellow schoolchildren, boys and girls. Not only did they not believe it either, but also they said that I was a child given to lying. With one voice they proclaimed, "We've never seen a sunflower dance."

Because classmates and friends didn't understand me I found no acceptance. I was disappointed and reluctant to go to school. A day passed, then a second and by the third I was even less willing to go.

My father wanted me to go, saying that I was the person in whom he had the most confidence and that I was brave. But I particularly wanted face and was afraid to go to school and be mocked by my classmates. My father said that I had to face up to this challenge and said so very firmly.

I wept, I resisted, I wouldn't listen to my father's advice; to a child this was an enormous matter. For the person I was then, apart from thieves, assassins, demons and monsters and being blown away by a typhoon, what else was there that was frightening? The most frightening of all was to lose dignity and to be afraid of the sneering looks of others.

My father thought of a way of encouraging me to go to school. He prepared two kinds of sweets for me. One kind was for the classmates who did not make difficulties for me and was a gesture of friendship and thanks, and the other kind was for the classmates who asked me why I hadn't been to school. These were called "gobstoppers."

With my father's encouragement I made my way fearfully to school. As was to be expected, I was met by a naughty boy who asked, "Why didn't you come to school? Are you a truant?"

I almost ran away but I remembered that I was the person that my father believed in most of all and steadied my mind and just gave him a sweet, saying in passing, "Have a sweet!"

The result was that he continued to ask and so I said, "Have a sweet," and stuffed another sweet in his mouth. I remembered what my father had said: this was called a gobstopper.

It was very effective and after a number of questions my classmates didn't seem too happy to pursue the matter. Later, even Little Banana forgot my dreadful "criminal record." In this way after I was rapidly reabsorbed into the class, it became a much treasured "school life regained" and I eventually achieved outstanding status in behavior and academic work.

Apart from the problems of life in my childhood I also had to face the deficiencies of the times. But it was my father who encouraged me to be courageous and happy.

The goodwill between people, their temperament and characters all suffered the influence of the times. But influenced more by a sense of family, the love of my mother and father never fell short. They were able to use their love to shield their children from storm and suffering and brought them up with a wonderful view of the world.

To have love in one's heart, to have goodwill and to have faith in both people and the world is, for a child, strength necessary to the process of growing up. The love, suffering and harmony within that strength are timeless and perpetual and once established are companions for life.

I am fortunate to have had a father with a heart of stone who gave me a sunlit childhood. His voice is always at my ear, telling me to remember that I am the person that he believed in most of all.

A Soft Voiced Father

I was very narrow-minded when I was young and this exercised my father who approached things very rigidly. As I gradually grew up and when I was at my most distressed I discovered that my father had become benevolent. He no longer lost his temper. He had become equable and spoke to me softly.

It was my second visit to the country with Mum and Dad to see my grandparents and Precious Chrysanthemum. On the way back we visited the seaside place on the map that my mother had so wanted to see. The sight of the sea and the sound of surf lifted our spirits.

An old lady was selling toys by the sea. There were a lot of toys and amongst them was a cloth-headed dog that, since the old lady had made it herself, had a name. It was called Crunch, the noise a puppy makes when it is chewing bones.

Crunch had a sweet smile, a straightforward character and seemed like pure spindrift from the ocean. I hugged Crunch to me and wouldn't let him go.

Mum said, "How good it would be if my daughter could

always smile like that."

Dad said, "True joy comes only from knowing love. Let her and Crunch be inseparable friends for ever."

During those few days Crunch and I were together every day and at night I went to bed with him in my arms, sleeping peacefully with love, the night filled with limitless warmth.

Sometimes, going to look at the sea at night, in the lightless space between street lamps I would fearfully look left and right, but all was well. I had the company of Crunch on both sides. I placed his little paws on my shoulders and no longer felt alone. It was good to have love and I didn't feel deserted.

I loved Crunch and thought that I would use my New Year money to buy him a smart cradle and a smart soft cap embroidered with a border of silver flowers.

In the depths of that very night there was a fire at the hotel where we were staying. The fire was fierce with thick smoke. I woke in alarm and felt for Crunch everywhere but couldn't find him at all.

It was my father who carried me out.

The fire brigade arrived. My father's luggage, left in the hotel, was scorched. Later, we searched everywhere but never found Crunch, the toy dog.

Mum walked and walked along the shore but never found the fairy-like old lady.

In tears, I said, "He's flown away."

Mum and Dad, with downcast countenance, said nothing, since not only had I been terrified by the fire, I had also lost a precious possession. They were perturbed and filled with anxiety. I was heartbroken and felt myself luckless, unable to protect my beloved Crunch.

The atmosphere of love is heavily tinged with suffering. When we reached home my father encouraged me to go and look at the flowers in the garden as a form of therapy.

"Don't cry. Don't be sad," my father said to me.

He softly told me that life was a process of perpetual gain and perpetual loss. For example, there was the loss of time, of treasured possessions and the loss of relatives. All this was heartbreaking, but it was a kind of spirit that was the most valuable of all. It was mankind's most wonderful joy, as sincere as the breath of the ocean.

I still wanted to cry.

Then suddenly and very tranquilly my father said, "You must remember that if there comes a day when I'm no longer in the land of the living, you must love your mother more than ever."

"Dad, why must you die too? I want you to go on living for ever." I wanted to cry again.

My father shook his head and said, "The finest flower withers, but once it's blossomed beautifully, isn't that a memory never to be forgotten?"

My father chatted with me and told me about my mother and how when he had no mother he had lived by himself, a bachelor with a head of hair like a hedgehog who smoked and, however you looked at it, could never be a father.

He drew his room for me. It was really, really terrible like an old storeroom. Inside there was a hammer, some shears and some old planks, a chipped tea bowl, a bowl of fish and several tortoises. There were dirty clothes everywhere.

Later he met my mother. He polished his shoes until they gleamed and because she was a beautiful red flower he wanted to marry her and take her home. My mother put out a beautiful tablecloth and set a warm table lamp where the tools had been. She also brought a gleaming tea set and spread a soft rug on the floor. The room became the best place in the world—our home.

Mother was a neat, cheerful woman who could write a good hand. Becoming her husband was a blessing for him.

Later, Mum became a mother and hid the child in her round belly where Dad could not find it if he tried.

Dad hammered away at the planks and made a little cradle and decorated it with little colored dogs and rabbits and corncobs and kites. His head was covered in wood shavings and his face was filthy, like a naughty elder brother, because at that time he still didn't know how to be a father.

Dad said that the day I was born was the happiest day of his life. He wanted me to believe that I was their dearest baby, the inexhaustible love that they had waited for.

He also said that at the time he had not known how to carry his daughter. He just knew how to say, "What fun, I'll sing her a lullaby."

Later, when I could walk he took me out to play and if he saw somebody he knew he would say, "Let me introduce you to my daughter."

When I was timid my father would say quietly in my ear that it would sound more impressive if I spoke up. He also took me to see the river where, sitting in a boat, he had emptied away that bowl of goldfish. He said that he had only realized when he had a daughter of his own that fish are happiest when they can swim where they want.

My father bought me some colored crayons, a whole pile of them. When he drew me he turned me into a most beautiful flower, saying that in his heart I was this golden ever-blooming flower.

My earliest drawings were all of my mother. I thought I had drawn beautifully but my father said, "Not like her at all, at all. The waist should be more slender and the eyebrows a little more curved."

I also drew my father, as a grim pile of stones and he said, "That'll do, that'll do. It looks quite fierce!"

I was deeply moved as I listened to my father's soft voice describing the emotion-packed family events of the past. I felt that although I had lost Crunch I was still enriched. I was not a luckless idiot and best of all, I had a mother and father who loved and cherished me.

At that moment I saw a plum blossom flowering beside me. My father pointed to it and said, "Little Fairy, this is your flower. It's yours and always will be. It's a flower to dream of, a lovely flower. Possess it and keep it in your heart for ever."

Throughout my childhood my father never once said anything weak or feeble to me. As long as he was there he always strove to rid my life of suffering and made me keep up my optimism, faith and love even when out of sight of the end.

Stories by Contemporary Writers from Shanghai